DREAM PAINTER

by
Paul Kersley
and illustrated by Joanna Roberts

HENDERSON

An imprint of DK Publishing, Inc.
Copyright © 1996 Dorling Kindersley Ltd.

"The circus tent rose into the night, a black dome silhouetted against a canopy of stars and blackness. Its arched entrance wide open, it was a Cathedral of Darkness..."

Chapter 1
"Four things to say…"

Twig tugged his hands from the pockets of his shorts and looked at his watch. He shrugged. He already knew the time, a minute had passed since he last looked. Shielding his gray eyes from the evening sun, he looked around.

Beneath red-tipped clouds, the flat park was empty. The wide-open iron gates through which no one came or went reminded him of his solitude.

He turned away, his loose shirt flapping like a sail.

And as the sun slipped down behind distant rooftop peaks, a thin wind followed him through the gap left by a missing post in the fence.

He had dared to enter another domain. At its center, rising above the tangled undergrowth with the magnificence of a forgotten castle, was a tall hut.

"Perhaps Budge is already here," his whisper met the heavy air. He checked, testing a much larger loose section of the fence to see if it had been disturbed.

"I hope he's been through," he wished, freeing his shirt from a snagging nail before setting off to wade through the weeds.

He aimed for the hut.

Right away panic began to boil up, ready to burst out. Lashing stems grabbed, the heady smell of leaves suffocated, he thought he was beginning to die, drowning, drawn under by the weeds. It did not matter. Twig forced himself to ignore everything, concentrating on pushing toward the hut. Keep looking at it, he knew he had to. A glimpse was enough, through the tangled branches. But if he lost sight of it he was sure he would struggle forever, never reaching anywhere.

It was that sort of place.

Finally he stood clear, shivering on a concrete slab at the hut's door. He listened.

There was the hush of a held breath.

His fingertips touched the handle. The wood was damp and he found himself staring at little pink spots of fungus.

"I'll risk it." He tugged the door.

Cold air poured out. The darkness remained inside.

Twig stood, waiting for anything to happen. Anything would tell him what to do next.

Twang. That sound came from somewhere within.

"Is that you Spike?" Twig's head darted, his ears trying to pick up more. It was too dark to see, too dark to risk going in. He moved aside from the door to let more light enter. It stretched far enough only to show a rusted watering can.

Twang.

"Spike," Twig heard his own yell, "I'm here."

"Yeh, yeh," a silly voice finally answered, "you're here. We know that. About time too."

"Well, you could have answered," Twig told him, taking one step in.

"Where you been?" Spike's stomach turned. "And why don't you just stroll in like the rest of us?"

6

"I was waiting, being careful," Twig didn't know why he bothered to speak. Spike was probably not bothering to listen. "Is Budge here?"

A shape in the gloom moved. It was heavy and large.

"Yeh," Spike sung. "Budge is here, I'm here, now you're here. If you shut the door we can get on with it."

Twig stepped further in, swinging the door shut.

Even before complete darkness could take over a candle was lit. While the waxy glow filtering through the cobwebs turned Spike's hair even more yellow, the flame spread a great shadow behind Budge. Budge sat, with baseball cap tipped low over his flat face.

Twang.

"I should have recognized that thing." Twig squinted at the elastic band stretched between thumb and forefinger of Spike's hand where he sprawled, elbow on the bench.

Twang. "Try and take it off me again then," came the jeer.

Twang.

Twig was tempted, poised but rubbing his wrist, remembering the wounds from the last time.

"I need to talk," Budge could just be heard.

But it made Twig come to the bench and sit on a buckling cardboard box. Spike put away the band, pulling his elbows off the table.

Both waited.

"I got four things to say." Budge spoke a little louder. "First…"

THE DREAM PAINTER

Twig cringed. He was in awe. The giant of school was pointing straight at him.

"First," Budge was saying, "you walk in here, free. Ain't no one else gonna use this hut while I use it."

"What about Crab?" Twig's skin crawled. He put his own hand around his throat at just the thought of their enemy.

"Crab wouldn't dare come anywhere near here," Spike nodded toward Budge.

"Second," Budge just continued from where he left off, "second, you gotta get yourselves more members. This gang's gotta grow."

"I saw Silk on my way here," Twig risked it, "think it would be great if…"

Twang, twang, twang…the elastic band interrupted.

"Silk!?" Spike protested to Budge.

"Yes, Silk," Twig dared, almost lunging.

"Come off it," Spike hollered, "she…" he shut up.

Budge was speaking.

"Third," Budge said, "Gotta get this gang a name."

"A name?" Twig heard Spike but he couldn't concentrate, couldn't listen.

"A name." Silk, he had said her name.

Silk.

He shut his eyes, even the candle was too bright. With eyes closed he could see her clearly.

Silk, she was on the footpath. She had been there when he came through the park's iron gates. With a sigh he remembered and could almost touch her now, her olive skin. And those eyes. But she was going the other way in her wheelchair, downhill, toward the trees, her black hair fanned down her back.

She had turned to smile.

Yesterday, she looked at him and today, she smiled.

Tomorrow? What would tomorrow bring?

"Tomorrow, we go to the circus."

"Wha…" Twig only just heard and opened his eyes, trying to concentrate. "What?"

"Knew you weren't listening." Spike hissed, "Budge just said his fourth thing. We go to the circus."

"When?"

"Tomorrow."

9

Chapter 2
"A good place to wait, a good place to meet"

Silk's eyes held a faraway look; they always did, as if seeing things from other times and distant shores.

She looked over her shoulder, about to call his name, but Twig had gone through the gates and was in the park, too far away to hear.

"Twig," her voice was musical, "it is a good name for you."

She smiled, even if he had not heard, at least she had spoken to him. Silk sat and watched him for a moment, his hurried strides leading him away until he became a dot. It was not difficult to know he was making his way toward the fence at the other side.

She wanted to follow, but it was late and there would be other times to talk.

He was the only one who showed her any kindness since she had joined the school. Somehow, she knew that a special friendship was beginning. She always knew such things. But special friendships take time to begin. She knew that, too.

Her hands on the wheel rims, Silk pushed down to start the chair moving.

Gravel crunched. It was easy going, the hedge-lined footpath led slightly downhill before it met the lane.

She hummed to herself, quietly, then became silent.

Someone was waiting.

A scarecrow by a lamppost, that was what he

looked like. The old man with scraggy hair stood in his overcoat.

She began to accelerate; she could not help it, the slope pulled her down toward him.

She was nearly there.

"Slow down," he quietly spoke.

And she did slow down. His voice, the same musical sound as Silk's, it seemed to slow everything.

"Grandfather." Silk coasted to him. She was out of breath, puffing a little. It made it hard to smile.

"You should not rush," he gently told her.

"But you must have been waiting a long time."

"It is a good place to wait," he soberly gestured to above the treetops, to where the last rays of the sun turned the sky copper.

She saw the deep sadness in his weather-tanned face and simply stated,

"He is coming, isn't he Grandfather."

"Yes," the old man nodded as he stepped behind the wheelchair and pushed up the lane toward the trees.

"Osmomso is coming," he said.

They walked into the dusk.

Chapter 3
"Don't laugh at the Clown…"

Osmomso knew what was going to happen.

In a flash a spotlight shone on him.

He blinked.
Dressed as a clown in baggy trousers, he stood on sawdust in the main ring of the circus.

Osmomso knew what would happen next.

The band's music bounced around the high tent, following "Osmomso-the-Clown," tumbling in circles, around and around, trying to keep up with the moving spotlight, the cheers and laughter following.
But it was the wrong sort of laughter.
They were laughing at him, not at the clown he was trying to be.
"You're not funny," someone jeered.
He kept going but eventually stalled to a halt. What to do? He tried a cartwheel, then stood. The last of the clinging sawdust fell away from his baggy trousers.
"Useless." He heard it so clearly from the crowd.
Osmomso spun, hands cupped as if expecting to be given something, only seeing face after face, laughing and laughing, straight at him.
All was spinning, faster and faster, a merry-go-round of dazzling spinning lights, colors,

and noise. Dizzy, he felt dizzy, putting his hands over his ears, trying to make it go away.

"Go away. Go away, you're just a dream," he knew and shouted above the din.

"A dream."

"A dream," his own shout shattered his sleep. He woke and sat straight up.

It was dark and silent. All gone. A dream.

The ticking clock was all he heard, "Ha ha-Ha ha" it said, the luminous face glowing in the dark.

Ten minutes to two, the hands made a smile. Even the clock laughed at him.

"Go away," he moaned.

Clasping his bald head with both hands, he sat in his dark bed, rocking back and forth, telling his mind to make it go away. It was only his mind playing tricks, he had to tell himself. It was his mind and the dreams of the night.

He felt that clammy night wrap itself around him.

With a grunt to shove it all aside, he reached for the matchbox and it rattled as his stubby fingers found it. Fumbling with shaking hands and spluttering matches, he managed to light the lamp on the bedside table.

The night was pushed away by the spreading glow, but so many nooks and crannies in the trailer left places where light could not reach. Those places, that was where laughter hid, ready to creep out into dreams. His mind told him that.

"Bah," he scoffed at it and his bald head glistened in the light as he rocked.

"All those kids," he growled, "looking at me,

laughing at me. Laugh at me. That's all they did."

"Kids, I'll teach them to laugh at me. I'll give them bad dreams, see if they like it."

All through the night, he sat, rocking back and forth in the bed of his trailer.

"Kids, I'll give them bad dreams."

All through the night Osmomso said it.

Chapter 4
"The Circus is in town…"

"Get your face painted. Line up."

The words skipped in the special time that fairgrounds and circuses bring. Even in daytime, even before things were all set up and opened, there was that magic.

"Line up." It came from the mouth drawn on the white painted face that floated like a balloon, not belonging to the announcer standing high on the bandstand, surrounded by half-built stalls and rides.

"Line up." But Twig was searching for Silk.

She was at the fairground, he had seen her for a fleeting instant. She moved so fast. And now he followed the wheelchair tracks in the dust.

"Line up." The call was filling his head, but it was the wheel tracks among the crowded patterns of kicked footprints that mattered most.

"Line up." Cursing and dodging, legs and dresses, sneakers and shoes, "Line up."

"Line up…Line up…" That call, trying to find Silk among the confusion, the whole thing was making him feel sick. "Line up…Line up."

Then he stopped. He had to stop, something, no, someone very wide blocked his path. A pair of rainbow laces, he saw that and knew. Slowly he looked up, right up, to a toothless grin.

"Crab." He said it.

But he should not bother to speak. Run.

Run!

Which way? In a rush he pictured the gap in the fence and the safety of the shed…too far, at the other end of the park.

Run!

He turned, darted, almost too late, too much time wasted thinking. Hands on long arms encircled him, trapped him, but he wriggled and slipped free. "Line up." Desperate, he ran to that call. "Line up," it was not a bad idea now. Everyone was obeying, forming a crowd, a good place to hide, squeezing through the mass of people that ended up at the line.

He could breathe again.

"Hey," someone had hold of his shoulder.

"No!" there was no room to run, he spun.

"Hi Twig." Twig slumped, he could never believe that he could be so pleased to see that yellow hair.

"Spike, Crab, he…"

"So?" Budge ambled forward.

Twig became calm, secure, with Budge in front and Spike behind. The line began to shuffle.

"Silk's here," he remembered and said it quickly, waiting to see what Budge would do.

"Yeh?" Spike danced in front. "*She* can't stand in line," he sniggered.

Twig wanted to hit him, but hardly moving, Budge gave him an elbow. It was a good one and Spike doubled over.

While Spike hopped and yelled more than he needed, Twig could guess the plan even before Spike cheated his way up the line.

"Some gang this is," Twig murmured.

But Spike was out of the way. That thump

he got from Budge though, it really showed Budge was on his side over Silk. He knew that now. And that was enough for the moment.

Moving behind Budge, trying to work out which part of the park they were on, he did not know it was his turn to go into the trailer until he saw the steps leading up to the open door.

Before he went in, he had to turn. He did not know why, he just had to.

High on the steps, he could see over the blank heads of the line.

Silk was in her wheelchair, aside from the rest. Her long hair swaying like grass, her head was moving from left to right, her lips mouthing one word.

"Don't."

"Don't," she was telling him as the moving line forced him deep into the trailer, leaving him just enough time to read the sign on the door.

"Osmomso, Face Painter."

Chapter 5
"Happy faces, happy dreams…"

All was stretched into slow motion for Twig.

It was a long, low corridor from the rear of the trailer to the dwindling daylight at the other end. Budge and Spike were waiting.

Two painted faces, two great big smiles.

His face must be the same because he saw them pointing at him. They bobbed with laughter.

Twig smiled and the drying paint made that smile stick. Then he laughed.

Laughter, howling by and bouncing from behind, came after him. He ran. He could fly. Twig launched himself at the other two, making them spill and tumble into the fresh air, the laughter roaring out over them.

In bursts of giggles between gulps of air they subsided on the grass, trying to untangle themselves.

"Osmomso's brilliant," Spike hollered as Twig figured out that the elbow wedged behind his ear was not his own.

"Let's see, see what we look like." Twig was the first to stand. He paid no heed to the stares of onlookers, thinning out aimlessly as the day ended and moonlight came.

Pink painted smiles stood grinning at each other.

It was difficult for Twig to recognize his friends, even with Spike's yellow hair sticking up and Budge's flat face beneath his baseball cap.

"Do I look different too?" Twig wished he had a mirror.

"Don't matter," Budge guffawed and slapped the other two on the back.

And it did not matter, nothing was important, nothing except laughing. And that laughter hung in the air around them like bubbles, bright and shiny.

"Hey," Spike exclaimed, "I can catch my own laughter." He gleefully jumped in the air. "It's great."

"What's happening?" Twig shrieked in fun. "These bubbles, our laughing, is this real?" Twig didn't really care, leaping up to grab the same empty space in the air as Spike.

"Hey, that's mine," Spike whooped.

"What are we doing?" Twig heard his own voice but did not really know if he was speaking.

"Spike, does my voice sound different?" His words echoed inside his head. "Hello," he shouted to test himself. "Hello," it rang in his ears.

"My face is numb," Budge moaned, slapping his face.

"Is it the faces," Twig asked, "making this happen?"

The whole thing was strange, weird. But no one seemed to care.

"I said it don't matter," Budge bellowed a laugh. He reached up high and over to grab a handful of air.

"Nothing matters any more," Spike agreed.

"We can do anything we like," Twig wasn't sure who had shouted.

"Who cares!"

Bursting, Twig and Spike acted together and hurled themselves at Budge.

"Get him, we're not scared."

Budge growled and dipped, easily chucking one over each shoulder. Gaining his balance like a triumphant weightlifter, he raised them higher in bouncing jolts.

It was unusual, being so high, but it began to hurt. Twig felt the pressure of Budge's arm around him; it was painful to laugh, hurting more with each bounce, bringing tears to his eyes, blurring his vision. Lights danced in front of his face.

He thought he saw something, a shadow. Fear unexpectedly arose from nowhere.

"Stop, stop," it echoed so many times.

"Stop, stop," was Spike calling, too?

They crashed. Twig bumped his nose on a pebble and felt the annoying pain of someone's boot on his shin.

With face buried, Budge still laughed. It seemed strange now, hearing Budge laugh. Spike joined in.

"Stop, stop," Twig shrieked then gave up and laughed. It became easy, just to lie there laughing, watching the bubbles rise.

"They are real, aren't they?" Doubt began to mix with the fear cropped up. He had seen something. He tried to focus his attention.

"Wait, wait," Twig's voice squeaked, trying to call out while rolling away from the others.

"Squeak, squeak," Spike mimicked.

Twig could see the funny side but forced himself to stand.

"Stop it." He crouched, grasping his knees,

trying to be serious, trying to start afresh.

"Crab." That shadow, Twig knew it was him. As he went through it in his mind, it became a vivid picture; a wide shape loping sideways.

"He's waiting."

"What are you saying?" Budge was groggy. He got slowly to his feet, wiping clods of soil from his cheeks, smudging his face paint.

"Oh no, not Crab," Spike was not bothered. He still lay facedown, clasping his hands behind his head, kicking rapidly. "Don't let him at me."

"But Crab," Twig spoke, not caring who listened, "while we were wrestling. I saw him."

When the truth unfolded, Twig instinctively ducked for cover behind a parked truck. He began to whisper to himself, wagging his finger with each word.

"It was him." He had to get his thoughts in order. "Behind that tent. Waiting for us."

He glared at Spike when he joined him, making sure he understood.

"You can't glare with a smiling face, Twig," Spike plainly told him. "It don't work."

"What's going on?" Budge could not be hurried; like a painted elephant, he strolled across.

Twig tried to focus. The dancing bubbles of laughter and his echoing voice had shrunk away. It left him all empty, but he had no time to think about it.

Over the heavy wheel of the sheltering truck, only outlines could be seen in the moonlight. Two loose ropes twisted out like serpents from the pyramid-shaped tent.

"I saw Crab sneaking behind."

The smell of gasoline and rubber teasing his nostrils, Twig regarded his friends. He saw two painted faces grinning in half darkness.

And he looked the same.

"Be serious," Twig insisted. Then he began to chortle, still not truly free from whatever was making things so funny. "No problem," Budge had awakened. Doubled over he hopped forward to the ropes. "C'mere," with hooked arm he called Spike, offering the spare rope.

"Go." Budge jabbed his finger to where he wanted Twig to go.

"What?" Twig could see what Budge wanted him to do. "You must be joking," his loud whisper was hoarse.

"Go on," Spike urged.

Twiddling his fingers, Twig gave a nervous giggle.

"Do it," Budge was convincing, even with that smile.

Shrugging, obeying, Twig walked by the pair and on toward the tent.

"I'll give the signal," Spike winked and jiggled his famous elastic band.

"Twig, put some effort into it," Budge hissed an order.

A comedy act, Twig put his hands in his pockets and whistled. But as he came alongside the tent, the back of his neck bristled.

What was he doing? Putting so much trust in his fellow gang members, without question.

"Spike," Twig squeezed back a shout. "Don't let me down," the situation was bringing on a fit of the giggles.

Twang, twang, twang.

Even before the alarm died a shape dived for Twig's ankles, but Twig was warned. He bolted only to stumble and fall. He closed his eyes and waited, dreading the worst.

One second stretched, almost snapping in two.

Was he alone, deserted?

"Come on then," he finally yelled, swallowing dirt.

A commotion followed. Someone screamed. It was awful. Was it Crab?

Twig raised his head from the ground to look back.

The scene was ridiculous.

Budge and Spike were doing a maypole dance around Crab, coiling him more and more in the ropes.

Twig flopped onto his back giggling in relief.

"You took your time," he shouted.

"Made it more fun," someone actually bothered to answer between the singing.

"Huh," Twig sniggered to the moon.

"He's escaped," Budge's sudden roar warned that Crab was free. Twig jerked, a reflex action. For an instant he thought Crab would grab hold of his ankles.

"Go on, get outta here," Budge growled.

"And don't come back," Spike added.

"I'll get you," Crab's distant scream faded.

Yes, Crab was free but safely away.

The fun must be over.

Twig closed his eyes. He needed time on his own. How tired he had become. Sleep approached rapidly. Without knowing it he was almost dozing, almost dreaming. He relaxed. He made himself relax, trying to find comfort on the hard ground. With the cool air drifting over his face, he heard the other two.

"Osmomso's brilliant," he recognized Spike's voice.

Osmomso... Twig realized, in the excitement he had not really seen the man. Twig had not paid attention while having his face painted, just eager to rush off and join the others.

"What happened?" he quietly asked himself.

Twig tried to think back, not clearly remembering being in, or leaving, the trailer.

"Was it the faces?" His question faded into space.

Nothing moved. Sounds drifted away, making the moon even more peaceful in a dark blue sky of torn clouds.

But Osmomso, what was he really like?

A cloud the shape of a toad slipped across the moon.

Twig could not help a shudder.

Twig awoke with a start. Something had slipped across a happy dream; something ugly.

In a flutter his eyes opened.

A white ceiling with fine cracks was spread above. He lay in his own bedroom. The weak light coming in through the yellow curtains told him it was dawn.

What had he dreamt?

Somehow he had gone home, that was obvious, but he didn't care. He was still tired.

As he rolled on his side, he giggled without knowing why, except that it hurt to laugh.

He lifted his head and groaned. All his muscles ached, but the pillow was smudged with colors and he had to know. Gently he touched his cheeks and felt the flaking paint.

"It's coming off…" Twig mumbled, his throat sore, "…need to go back…need to see Osmomso."

Chapter 6
"The call of Osmomso cannot be denied…"

The night air was electric at the street corner. Beyond Twig could see the whole park with the fair fully installed. It floated in the darkness, a bizarre ocean liner with lights ablaze.

The beat of the disco sounds from the rides clashed horribly with the traditional organ tunes. The chaos of music spread out through the park gates to wind around the streets.

Following a pied piper's call, the crowds came. They barged past Twig leaving him feeling as if he did not exist. So rude, he did not really want to join them.

But he had to have his face painted again.

So, hands in pockets, he paced into the park and onto a black strip of grass. It was a no-man's-land, where the lights of the streets never touched and the fairground lights could not reach. He was walking on stars and the patterns of lights the rides cast across the ground.

Engrossed, he was within the fairground before he knew it, surrounded by the whizz of noise and bustle.

The circus tent stood like a landed UFO in the center. He avoided it without knowing why. It held something for him, a dreadful memory of a long-dead past, or the premonition of something to come. If he was asked he could never explain.

He just avoided it.

Walking past cotton candy clouds and

stuffed toys clutched in arms, he made his way to Osmomso's trailer. A magnet, it drew him away from the fun to a dark corner.

There was no warning. Twig's brain leaped forward a step. A string of events happened rapidly, leaving no time to react until it all passed.

Silk whooshed in front of him. She stopped quickly, almost flying headlong out of her chair.

"Do not go in," she said firmly, without ceremony.

"Wha…?" Twig slurred, reeling. Silk was there. She was there, close, and she was talking to him.

"Don't," her eyes were wide. "Don't go into Osmomso's trailer. The dust of the dead will…"

"Hey, Twig," someone bumped into him.

"Let's go before a line builds up." It was Spike, he was leading him away by the arm.

"Wait," Twig dug in his heels.

Silk had spoken to him, so simply. And he thought it would involve time and planning in the playground before they could ever have a chance to speak to each other.

What was she telling him though?

"Dust of the dead?" he murmured.

"C'mon, Twig," Spike was dragging him away.

Silk pleaded with her eyes. Twig started to reply but could only stare down at her face, half hidden by her long hair, her legs in a blanket, her hands delicately holding the wheels of her chair. And those eyes.

"Twig," Spike insisted, "come on."

"Let go," Twig shook free. "Stop bossing me around. I'm always being bossed."

Twig stood rocking, unsteady on his feet. He wanted to speak to Silk. It was his chance. His heart began to pound, his throat dried. Silk was gliding nearer with scarcely any effort.

"I…" words could not form for Twig.

A great shape appeared out of the background.

"Hey Budge," Twig heard Spike's greeting.

Budge just walked by, a zombie, ignoring everyone.

"What's wrong, Budge?" Spike whined.

"Need to get my face painted," Budge replied flatly.

"C'mon," Spike grabbed Twig again. "Catch up with Budge."

"I…" Twig still could not speak.

A whisper formed inside his head, a silent call no ear could ever hear. He was being summoned, called by something dark and powerful which he knew was in the trailer.

"Need to get my face painted." Was Budge responding to that same call?

"Don't," Silk's word shimmered and disappeared.

In a dream, he let himself be pulled away. Silk became smaller as the distance between them grew. Perhaps she would eventually fade into nothing. Now someone else was beside her. He came from the shadows, as if it was shadows from which he was made.

"Who?" Twig hooted.

With scraggy hair, a scarecrow in an overcoat moved into the light, closer to Silk.

"Who?"

Dazed, he turned and followed Spike and Budge up the steps. Once more Twig went into Osmomso's trailer.

Chapter 7
"Twisted smiles, twisted dreams.."

Sucked into the trailer, drawn, not by Spike's bullying, but by a dark and silent call, Twig no longer felt the pull of Silk or the mystery of the old scarecrow.

He was there, in Osmomso's trailer. He was there again. He had been there before yet he remembered nothing of it. Why? He did not think to question.

But where were Spike and Budge, Osmomso?

Nothing moved but Twig could feel the tension tighten like a coiled spring.

He could only guess the size of the trailer. Clad in purple curtains, the edges just faded into softness. A purple cloud.

In a far end he could see a bed. A throne, it dominated the space.

Everything was silent.

Among the cloud, Twig was surrounded by the everyday clutter of clothes, dishes and chairs. All so powerful, alive. Each object jealously owned the place it occupied. The dim light did the same, and so did the shadows – especially the shadows. Everything had a special place where no stranger dare intrude.

Twig was intruding.

Where were Spike and Budge, Osmomso?

He dare not call out.

But from somewhere began a deep mumble. It grew louder rising to fill the air, a demonic chant turning into a single laugh. It ended abruptly. With a swish, an arrow of light flew and Twig could see clearly. In front of the light's source, Budge was leaving a cubicle formed by a curtain.

"Budge," Twig wanted to collapse into his arms.

The curtain swished again as it was drawn wider, and now the glare made it difficult to see properly.

"Feels good, I'm better now," Budge emerged as if dancing to reggae music. "Spike's nearly done, then it's your turn."

Closer, Twig saw him properly. Budge's thumb was telling him to go into the cubicle.

"But Budge, your face!"

Twig gaped at the green painted face. That smile. It held so much pain, so much torture.

"Feels good, it's cool," Budge nodded his reassurance.

That deep mumble began to rise again. Twig thought it was Budge but it definitely came from the cubicle. The glare made it impossible to see inside. Twig wanted to run.

"In you go," Spike was suddenly there, catapulted out and forcing Twig in.

"But..." Twig tried to protest, trying to slow things. "Spike, your face, it's like Budge's. How can a smile be so horrible?"

"Feels good," Budge was leaving, not involving himself.

"Go on, it's your turn," Spike said, threateningly pushing Twig toward the chair.

A tug of war in reverse, Twig resisted but felt himself weaken. He briefly sensed a chance to escape. Spike, too, seemed to weaken and his hold slipped.

Then he saw why.

"Osmomso," he heard Spike's worship.

A huge mass, much larger than Budge, was standing in front of the light.

"Come in," the syrupy voice was enticing.

"See," Spike was agreeing. "It's all right, go in."

Twig's legs carried him into the cubicle. It was warm and humid. He sat staring at the array of small paint jars spread over the table. He felt, rather than saw Osmomso enter, and heard the curtain swish shut.

Now Osmomso was sitting opposite, dressed in a purple gown, his bald head glistening, a golden glow.

"There," Osmomso reassured, "nothing to worry about."

And there was nothing to worry about. Twig saw the brush stir the paint, and going cross-eyed watched it approach his face. The green goo dripped on the table. It felt warm on his cheek.

"Feels good," he heard himself say.

"Of course it does," Osmomso nodded deeply.

Twig watched the thick eyebrows arch as Osmomso concentrated, intent on his art. He felt the paint spreading over his face, forming a moist mask. Now his lips were being painted and he felt his own lips forming a smile. Then he saw the smile of Osmomso; a twist of cruel satisfaction.

"Aahh," Osmomso let out a long breath.

"All done," he nodded. His body began to

quiver, a drooling laugh was building up.

"Go now," Twig was dismissed by a flick of a stubby finger. "Enjoy your dreams then come back for more."

Osmomso's laugh wrapped around Twig as he left the cubicle. The purple trailer was not threatening now. Shadows slunk out to welcome him, embrace him, making him a part of the interior.

Twig did not want to leave, so pleasant was the sensation. He could stay there forever, with Osmomso.

"You look good," Spike greeted him at the doorway.

In the late night carnival atmosphere seeping in the aroma of hot dogs and onions, Twig was properly reunited with Budge and Spike.

"Your faces don't seem so bad now," he shouted above the racket.

"Feels good," Budge danced in a space clear of people.

The air felt cool through Twig's clothing but the warm sensation of his face spread over his whole body, creating a tingling numbness.

"Glad I had it done again," Twig said.

"See, told you," Spike walked away.

"Are we going?" he shouted, trying to keep up with the other two. They were merging with the crowds.

"Where are you?" He had lost them.

The crowds began to close in, a squeezing mass of heads and shoulders. He was lifted off the ground and never fell. The grip was so tight it supported and carried him to where he did not want to go – the giant dome of the circus tent.

"Let go," he twisted, forcing himself clear by an act of will. Coarse fabric of people's coats grazed his hands as he struggled, pushing his way through, until he stood in the side ground, scared to even look at the circus tent.

"Why?" No answer came.

The bright lights, the music, and the calls of the barkers. Twig wanted no part of it. He craved the shadows. Darkness called him. He no longer belonged with people, they were beginning to notice him.

Someone looked at him and backed away. More did the same. A little girl pointed and screamed, clutching her mother. Twig saw the accusing glare in the mother's eyes.

"Is my face that bad?" He did not dare touch it.

"I want to go home." He began to leave.

Looking down, ashamed to show his face, he saw the ground pass by beneath. He left the area of the showground and walked over the kaleidoscopic patterns thrown by the fairground lights, remembering them from when he had entered the park.

Then darkness came.

He was in the strip of no-man's-land. That blackness begged him to stay, enticing him to another world, deep and never-ending, a world where he would wander alone for eternity.

Sensation was returning to his body, the numbness was passing. He felt cold, alone, and afraid.

"Budge, is that you?"

Someone was there, Twig was convinced.

"Spike?" Any moment Twig would hear the *Twang* of the elastic band. He prayed he would.

Laughter came, mocking. Not from outside, but from within. The same laughter he had heard from Osmomso, the same laughter that would fit the painted smile of Budge and Spike. The same laughter that came from his own painted smile.

He was laughing with the darkness, he heard himself, a cruel laughter that he could not control and from which he could not run.

Still he ran. He fled into a nightmare journey, into the orange glow of the streetlights that showed no comfort, only twisting streets of mocking laughter.

Twig lay in his bed, the crazed pattern on the ceiling above.

"You should eat," his mother's voice came up the stairs.

"Not hungry," he mumbled.

"Well, have you washed your face?"

Twig did not dare touch his face, not understanding how paint could hold so much power.

He turned on his side and gently cried.

Twig opened his eyes, the cool air touched his face. The dark blue night sky was clearer now. The toad-shaped cloud had slid far from the moon and was at the horizon.

"A dream?"

He lay outside on the grass in the park amidst the half-erected fairground.

"Osmomso's brilliant," Spike's shout drifted across.

Twig lifted his head. At eye level with the silvery moonlit ground, he saw Spike and Budge still cavorting in the tent's ropes.

"Shhh," Budge could never whisper, Twig heard him clearly.

"You'll wake him."

"I am awake," Twig shouted, "been dreaming."

He saw Budge and Spike's pink painted smiles and smiled back.

"A silly dream." Twig groaned happily and flopped onto his back, an arm hooked over his forehead.

"Look out!" Spike's shout came.

"What!"

Too late Twig recoiled. Manacles of cold hands grabbed his ankles.

"Crab's back," Budge roared.

"Help," Twig pleaded. He could not struggle free. The grip around his ankles was too tight, he was being dragged away.

Spike and Budge could never reach him now.

The rough ground forced his clothes to ride up. His bare skin scraped by the ground, he was being dragged away to be skinned and eaten alive.

His breath came in short gasps. The moon passed by above, inch by inch.

Inch by inch he was going to die.

His own rasping breath woke Twig.

"Oh no," he groaned at the ceiling.

He lay in his own bedroom. Once again it was dawn. His green painted face was tired and drawn.

"Oh no," he was fed up. "What part of a dream is this?"

"Mine!" A roar filled the room.

Dawn went, darkness returned. Two arms rose from beneath the foot of the bed.

"Huhh," Twig sucked in his breath and drew in his legs.

But he was caught. A grip of cold, hard bone tightened around his ankles, pulling down. Inch by inch he was being dragged away, his pajamas riding up his back with the friction of the bottom sheet.

The cracks in the ceiling slipped away.

His brain yelled at his body to do something.

Desperately he grabbed at the bedpost, fingertips clutching on. He reached further and strengthened his hold.

"You won't get me," he hissed. He was fighting back, "you won't get me, Crab or whoever you are."

His grip was holding, he could win.

"Ohhh," he moaned.

His body was beginning to stretch, inch by inch, his arms first, then his legs.

The ceiling slipped away again, inch by inch. He lay looking at it in the gray light of an approaching dawn.

He was being pulled down to the dark world beneath the bed, his limbs stretched and impossibly bent. Joints popped and bones cracked, twisted the wrong way. Pain burned its way up his spine. Time stopped, it became an endless torture.

"No!" His scream split the night, slicing the nightmare open.

All night long, Twig sat on his bare bed shivering, his arms around his legs hunched up to his chest.

He did not dare to sleep.

His painted face, with a green smile, was twisted horribly by the moonlight streaming in past the curtains.

Chapter 8
"Osmomso's shadow can stretch far…"

The fairground was dead and silent, hanging limp beneath a wet, gray sky. It was Sunday morning, everyone was sleeping and nothing moved except the litter swirled by the wind.

With black bomber jacket zipped up to the chin, Twig clung to the park gate. His scrubbed face felt raw, his fingers turning blue with cold. A north wind skimmed the hedge-top of the footpath and wove in and out through each railing. He did not want to let go of those railings, no matter how cold he was. If he let go a morning's dream might snatch him away like litter.

The wind tried to snatch him away, coming in gusts, taking away all thoughts, taking away all sounds.

"Twig," he thought he heard something but perhaps he dreamed the call. He was tired and had little energy.

Silk was there.

She was tilted forward in her chair, leaning into the wind, her brown hair flowing behind as if she was flying, free.

"How are you?" She was shouting above the wind, looking up to his face.

"What?" He could hardly hear and without thinking, wearily bent his knees, dropping to move closer to her mouth.

"I asked how you were," she called. He felt her breath on his cheek in the wind.

Those eyes were melting him.   She was

speaking to him so easily and he was tongue-tied, trying to pull himself away from sleep.

"Oh...er," Twig realized she was waiting for an answer. "Er...I'm fine," he lied.

He felt only numbness.

"You look tired," she told him.

Twig just shrugged, wanting to snuggle into the comfort of her tasseled blanket and cry himself to sleep. She seemed warm and he was cold and empty.

"He is a bad man," Silk plainly said.

"Who?" Twig's forehead furrowed. He drew back.

"You know who." It was obvious she did not want to say his name. Twig could see her faltering, almost showing fear.

"He has stolen the power," she was grave. "The dust, it should not be used this way."

"I don't know what you're talking about," Twig's mind was in a turmoil.

"It does not matter for now. But you have to be strong, Twig. Find your strength," her determined words were telling of her own strength. "Or you will lose your soul."

"My soul...how..?" He darted his eyes away and stared vacantly at the ground, hiding. This was not the conversation he ever wanted with Silk. All the things he had once planned to say: harmless talk, "Where are you from?" "Hamburgers and MTV" so far away now.

It was then he felt alone.

Her bare arm stretched out from beneath her blanket. Silk reached for his hand then changed direction. Twig felt her lightly touch his face, stroking his cheek. He blushed and felt goose bumps forming.

"I have to go," she immediately released the brake and shoved herself down the path.

Twig remained stooped, and felt his own hand stroking his face, as she had done.

The footpath dipped quickly and she was gone.

He had to follow.

Twig knew she lived nearby, she came that way to school. Moving to the top of the incline, he could see the entire length of the path and she was halfway down, coasting.

"Why don't I just go with her, push her in her wheelchair?" He had never thought of pushing her.

"No, I'll follow." He crouched, hiding, waiting until she was a safe distance away.

It was helping him, the daring, the thrill of tailing someone.

Bad dreams were going away.

🦇 🦇

Osmomso squatted on the chair; it was too small for his large bulk. In his cubicle, the curtains around him created a purple tent from which the stale air and warmth could not escape. Sweat began to ooze from his skin. The bare light bulb spread its naked glow, illuminating everything. The table was covered with jars of colors.

He was preparing his paints for the night.

🦇 🦇

Looking down the two long straight lines created by the hedge, Twig saw the distant figure standing near the streetlight before the trees. He knew right away that he was the scarecrow who met Silk at the fairground.

Silk was eager to meet him, Twig could tell. She was speeding up. So Twig knew he was not a threat.

"I should be a detective when I leave school." Bad dreams slipped away. He was trying to feel better, glad he was doing something on his own for once, without having to rely on the approval of Budge, or being pestered by Spike.

The gang was okay, but this was better.

He watched Silk and the old man meet. They spoke. Twig ducked. Silk was pointing up toward him, they must be talking about him.

Stroking his cheek again, Twig felt vulnerable.

"Perhaps Budge should be here," he thought. "What is she telling him about me?" He clutched at the ground and found little comfort in the cold gravel.

The old man moved gracefully behind Silk and pushed her up the lane. They were out of sight.

Twig acted fast. He had to sprint down the path to be sure he did not lose them.

Faster and faster, segments of hedge sped past his field of watery vision. The cold wind was making his eyes water and blasted his cheeks, he knew they were turning red, they were burning. He began to wheeze, his head turned from side to side as he ran. Nausea boiled up in his stomach.

But he had to keep going. There was no chance of stopping anyway, the path was too steep and he was running too fast.

The streetlight loomed closer, cold and hard. He aimed for it, praying he could use it as an anchor to halt and support him, or else he would crash into the trees.

Flat palms slapped, stinging, he was inches away from smashing into the streetlight. But he managed to hold on. Coughing, taking gulps of cold air and trying not to collapse, he had not showed enough sense to swing to the side and cut down the risk of being seen.

They were not far up the lane. He had a chance to recover.

But they were turning a curve.

It was time to move, no time to rest.

With legs like jelly he began to follow, loping, half running, half walking. He had to trust they would not look back since the wire fence alongside meant he could not dive into the trees for cover. At the curve ahead they moved off the lane and through an entrance almost arched by overgrown rhododendrons.

He neared the entrance and crept stealthily, trying to hold his breath. A dirt track full of potholes and puddles struggled through the trees – a forest glade dappled lime-green.

They were gone.

"I wonder," Osmomso licked his thick lips, "Are they in my power yet?"

He bent his torso down so that he could use a key on a chain around his neck to open a drawer beneath the tabletop. He groped inside for an earthenware jar.

"I wonder."

Into each jar of mixed paint he sprinkled just a pinch of ocher dust from the earthenware jar.

Twig crept into the wooded walkway.

Tossed about by the strengthening wind, the trees rustled excitedly. They were whispering about him, passing the message along, from tree to tree.

Heavy clouds roamed the strip of sky above the road.

A dark storm was coming.

Osmomso used the stem of a paintbrush to stir and stir each jar of paint. It slurped.

"Bad dreams are coming," he drooled.

The trees were closing in, becoming dense. A crisscross of heavy boughs formed a tunnel, with shadows turning stronger as the storm approached.

Head moving, searching side to side with each step, Twig paced further up the road.

Osmomso stopped stirring and lined up the jars of dribbled colors, watching his shadow spread as his hand passed over the last one. The color was black.

Twig felt his back crawl, something was behind him. He felt it, seeing it in his mind; a creeping presence, a shadowy hand reaching out to grasp his shoulder.

He turned.

Nothing. Trees began to creak as branches rubbed. The wind was increasing.

He walked again, moving further up the road into the woods.

"Who..?" He whipped about, convinced he was being followed.

Standing still, Twig could see the arched entrance through which he had come.

Finding Silk was not so important now.

But something was there again, still there. Behind him. It was behind him, no matter which way he turned.

Shaking, almost bursting with a swallowed scream, he used all his willpower to stand still, not allowing himself to turn endlessly, not allowing himself to be bullied by whatever was behind him.

It was black. He knew it was black, and it was coming closer. And he was standing there letting it happen.

"No." He screamed, denying what he was feeling.

"You are not here." He heard his shout die in the trees.

"You are not here."

But still he could not help but lash out, turning and backing away with no direction until he jammed himself against a tree trunk.

He clung onto the coarse bark, it was real.

Whimpering like a puppy, he prepared himself to let go and run, sizing up the distance to the arched entrance which meant escape.

Could he make it?

*   *

"I will wait for the night."

Osmomso had finished. He treasured the jar of dust before returning it to the drawer, and grunted with the effort of bending so that the key on the chain would reach the lock.

Switching off the light he left his cubicle and the paint jars standing in darkness.

*   *

Fear retreated as quickly as a light being turned off. Twig felt a sense of relief, tinged with shame at how he behaved when nothing was really there.

"I just imagined it," he convinced himself.

Chapter 9
"Many truths will be told, tonight…"

Its feathers smooth and gray, a bird dipped its tail and flew from the mossy ground. It sought refuge on a low, lichen-covered branch. Silk watched its round eye regarding her.

"Twig was frightened, Grandfather."

Silk felt secure, even as the wheelchair rolled over the clumps of grass and through the trees. Overhanging branches brushed over her as she passed through, and green snowflakes of falling leaves clung to her hair.

Her grandfather confidently pushed her back onto the dirt road.

"We could have helped him," she said. "Wasn't it wrong to just hide and watch?"

"No," Silk heard the steady voice from above and behind. "He has to find his own strength. That is the way it should be."

Silk knew not to question his wisdom, but it did not remove the pity she felt for Twig.

She was being pushed smoothly along the road, her grandfather avoiding all the holes and bumps. Tilting her head back, Silk looked at the canopy of trees and then at the sky.

The storm never came.

"But what was scaring him?" Silk asked.

"Bad dreams awakening." She knew the old man would say no more about Twig until another time.

"But, Grandfather. What will we do now?"

"We must wait. We can do nothing but wait. We shall know what to do when the time arrives."

Fresher than the perfume of the woods, the air about them cleared, rising up to an open sky. They had entered a circular clearing, occupied by a converted barn, its chimney smoking.

"It is nice being here with you," Silk slowly smiled away her troubled thoughts. "But, Grandfather," she hesitated, "Do you miss your proper home?"

"Home?" He was proud. "What American Indian has a home? It was stolen from us so long ago."

"Hah," she laughed strangely, "but you are still a true Brave. You lost Twig so easily."

"Yes," he agreed. "But we shall talk with him soon. I know you want us to."

"And it was easy to lose him, because it was easy to know he was following. Our fathers and their fathers pass such knowledge down."

"Tell me about your grandfather," Silk asked, her words filling the clearing. They were nearly home. "Was he really a Chief?"

"Yes," he answered. "And I shall tell you many things tonight. It is time for that."

Chapter 10
"Nightmares are coming…"

"What are we sitting in this old dump of a shed for?" Spike snapped. "Let's go. Go and get our faces painted. It's time."

Twig shivered and huddled closer to the candle's flame, wanting only to soak up every flicker of light.

"Budge is the boss," Twig spoke without thinking. But he meant it.

"Your mommy's looking for you," Spike jeered. He fidgeted, edgy, drumming his fingers on the tabletop. He was worse than ever.

"I'll go home when I want," Twig tried to boast but didn't try too hard. Spike didn't matter any more.

Being in the hut was all that mattered. It was a cocoon, safer than anywhere else.

"Spoke to Silk earlier," he said it to try and console himself. "Lost her…" his voice faded.

The candle's light could not reach the bare boards at his feet. Miserably, Twig looked down.

It was a black hole. In despair, he wanted to tumble into it.

Silently he wished that he had not lost Silk, wanting to be with her. Coming away from the woods was hard, but he could not have lingered. Shadows would reach for him.

He had not gone home. Skirting the fairground he had crossed the park. Only the security of the shed had made him come through the fence and battle the weeds. Only the security of the shed. And Budge.

"C'mon Budge," Spike was nudging, "let's go."

Budge was not speaking, just sitting. Twig became aware of this and stared.

Sullen, with sunken cheeks, Budge was not moving.

"Budge…" Twig dared whisper, "…do you have nightmares…do you dream…when you are awake…nightmares…?"

"Shut up," Spike intervened, obviously agitated by the subject of nightmares. "C'mon Budge," he pushed, "I need to get my face painted. It might make my dreams go away."

"Do you have them, too?" Twig, oddly, felt sympathy for Spike.

"Shut up," saliva flew from Spike's mouth. "Come on, Budge," he shook him irritably, "you need to get your face painted."

"Need to get my face painted," Budge merely agreed.

"…I have nightmares…" Twig finished what he was saying, speaking to himself, "I have nightmares…when I'm awake…"

The candle went out.

Twig was being drawn into the blackness.

"…Need to get your face painted…" a mocking voice filled his mind, "…painted faces, painted dreams…" it mingled with mocking laughter.

Nightmares were coming.

"…Come on you two…" Spike's distant words echoed through.

Following the echoing words and laughter out of the shed, drowning in tangled weeds, passing through shadows blurred by lights and musical noise, past a bland mass of people,

Twig entered a cloud of purple haze.

He blinked, awakened from his dream.

Shivering alongside the figure of Budge, Twig recognized the purple shrouded interior of Osmomso's trailer.

"I brought them for you," Spike was saying. "Now will you make my dreams go?"

Twig saw. Osmomso sat, a smiling fat toad, his tongue ready to flick out and draw him in.

Chapter 11
"Where eagles soar and ghosts dance..."

From the bandaged stovepipe, wood-smoke leaked and curved up, dodging beneath the oak beams in the high roof. As it spread everywhere, the smoke left behind a little of its stain. With this happening every day, year after year, the whole room developed sepia tones. The walls, the dusty furniture, and even the shaft of daylight beaming in, all held the quality of an aging photograph.

Protected from the stone floor by a gaily colored, woven rug, Silk nestled against the leg of her grandfather's chair. He was sitting comfortably in his faded corduroy suit and tattered slippers.

She adored being there, listening. His tales often carried them to faraway places, distant shores, and distant times.

The pleasing scent of wood-smoke wafted over her.

"Is this why they call you Woodsmoke, Grandfather?" she gently teased.

"There are many reasons for a name," his steady voice vibrated through the chair. Silk could both feel and hear him speak.

"Many reasons for a name," tilting her head, Silk smiled to herself.

"It is a good name for you though," she laughed and then sighed. She had said the same thing about Twig. "But you were going to tell me many things tonight, Grandfather. Is it time?" She frowned. "What are we going to do? About you? About us? We must help Twig."

His weathered hands gently stroked her hair. Sliding closer, she prepared herself to listen to his tale.

He was going to talk for a long time. This she knew.

"It has been many years since I first came to this land," he said. "I was here during the war and I stayed."

"You were a war hero," she reminded him, without really knowing what that meant.

He did not respond immediately. "A circus star, I was called," he quietly laughed. "I could wander aimlessly with the circus. It was enjoyable, but in truth I was only another animal act, doing cheap stunts."

"No," she would not believe it.

"A drugstore Indian," he said. "That would be the expression in what was once our own land. But I did it because of my promise to look after you. And I was proud to do so."

"Does it hurt to drown?" Silk had never asked before.

"Your father and mother died together. That would be important to them. Knowing that, it is easier for us to carry on."

She ran her fingers over his ragged slippers. "And you became like an animal act, to make money, to look after me?"

"That is not important," he answered.

"But…" she stopped. Silk knew that Grandfather's way would be correct.

"You understand so much," he comforted her. "You will understand much more as you grow."

"I was going to be a circus star like you," Silk quietly touched her own legs and felt nothing.

"I know," he said sadly. "Yet that, also, is not important. Do not think my words unkind."

"I trust you," she consoled him.

"And for now," he said firmly, "we must deal with the present problem."

"Osmomso," she whispered, "our dust."

"It is neither ours nor his," he said. "It is our fathers and their fathers."

"Tell me again," she said eagerly.

Silk was carried away, over oceans and grassy plains, to desert mountaintops, of sunset-red and ocher.

A place where eagles soar and ghosts dance.

"Before I left America," he said, "I was allowed to carry with me a pot of dust. It belongs to the place where our ancestors roam, the place where our earthly bodies are laid to rest."

"But what does it do," she asked, "carrying the dust with you?"

"It means we may easily bring our spirit guides with us," he explained. "We may wander aimlessly without a home in this world, but with the dust, the spirits will have a home wherever we are."

"Ghosts should not be allowed to wander aimlessly," she recalled.

"Yes," he agreed, "our spirit life is sacred, more important than our time on this earth.

"Yet we must endure with dignity while we are here, so that we may be proud spirits. That is why it is not important that I performed cheap circus acts. This is why it is not important that my son, who was your father, drowned with your mother. And, Silk, that is why it is not important that you cannot feel your legs. We must endure with dignity."

"I try, Grandfather," she said painfully. "But sometimes it is hard."

"Yes of course," he had stopped stroking her hair but started again.

"I try," she quietly repeated.

"I know. Yet for now we must think of the dust of our ancestors. It is sacred."

"And he stole it," Silk scowled.

"Yes, and with an evil mind, it can do evil deeds."

"Yes," she whispered privately, becoming distant. Silk stroked her legs and looked up into the shadows of the high roof.

"Do not linger with bad memories," he said.

"No," Silk was determined to steer all thoughts away from self-pity.

"Only the dust matters," she vowed.

"It is true," he nodded. "We must retrieve it from him. Without it my spirit will roam, and when I die, I will also be lost. And while it is used, a little of me dies."

She suddenly moved and hugged his legs.

"You won't die," she assured him. His legs were so thin. She had hugged him only days before and since then he had lost weight, fading away.

"And while it is used, a little of me dies," he said it again. "I must get the dust back soon."

"You won't die," she said firmly, trying to understand all that had been said.

"So," she continued, "Osmomso uses the dust in the paint, and it affects those he paints?"

"It gives them dreams," he added. "It becomes a drug. It is addictive. They will always want more."

"So we must save them," Silk knew. "We have to get the dust to save Twig and his friends."

"Or they will become lost souls," he continued for her. "My soul will be lost with theirs."

"I see…" she could say no more, not dwelling on the fate of her grandfather.

"I trust you," she told him again.

"Twig must be strong," he added, "so that his soul is strong enough to fight back."

"How did Osmomso know about the dust?" she suddenly wondered.

"He saw it, when I was in the circus and when he was a clown. He asked, and I told him how our fathers' fathers painted their faces. He was anxious to use it with his own makeup but I would not let him."

"Then he tricked you and stole it," Silk said it for him.

"Yes. We must trick him and get it back. We must do it soon."

"Perhaps Twig can help us."

"If he can be strong."

"But you said our fathers used to paint their faces?" Silk was catching up with so many explanations.

"Our fathers and their fathers, they knew how to," he said. "It was used in war paint."

"Ahh," she nodded. "War paint. And the dust helped?"

"So it is said," he stated.

"And now Osmomso uses it for face painting," she understood a little more.

"Painted faces, painted dreams."

"How?" she asked.

"Even the dead must dream."

Chapter 12
"How long will this dream last?"

Twig stood at the shed's door beneath a clouded moon.

He did not know how he came to be there.

It was raining. Water dripped from the shed's roof and ran in glossy miniature rivers to form a puddle in the worn concrete at his feet.

In the puddle he saw the rippled reflection of a darker world, where tree limbs stretched over the sky to form fingers clutching at the moon.

And he saw his own reflection, and his painted face.

"Ugh," he sucked in his breath.

Bat's wings, the black paint was spread at angles over his cheeks, with a mouth of white teeth grinning across a skull of sunken eyes.

He prayed his face was just painted, and that this was not how it was going to be forever.

But he was about to be chased. He knew. Haunted by anything such a painting could conjure up; nightmares of all the demons from hell.

"No use running," he knew, "need a safe place to hide."

He pulled at the shed's door, it refused to open.

He pulled harder, it seemed to activate a lever, a grating sensation vibrated up through his boots. The concrete slab was moving. A trapdoor, it fell away taking him with it.

"It can't be," his feeble words trailed off forever.

Into a sea of noise and images, he plunged.

Wings of blood-red bats darted at him, messengers bringing distant screams of torture.

He spiraled, no longer falling, rather drifting, through pinpoints of stars, into a cloud of purple mist.

The mist was clearing, gathering in one place to form a solid shape.

Twig sat, with no option but to accept his fate, knowing what the shape was forming, knowing where he was and what was happening.

The last of the mist receded.

"Osmomso," the bald head leered at Twig. Beneath a bare light bulb, Twig was in the confines of the cubicle having his face painted.

"There is no escape," Osmomso said smoothly. He was sticking his brush into a jar of what could have been black treacle. "No matter what you dream," he nonchalantly dabbed at Twig's face with the laden brush, "you will always come back to me from now on."

"Is this a dream?" Twig heard what sounded like his own voice, but he wasn't sure. "Is this a dream?" He was asking again.

"What is a dream, and what is real?" Osmomso teased as he dipped his brush again. "Just accept that you will stay with me. Don't fight it, just make it easy for yourself."

Twig pulled away from the approaching brush. It felt and smelled revolting, the stench of a rotting corpse.

"Do you want to taste it?" Osmomso was dribbling.

"No." Twig leaped through the cubicle. In two steps he reached the curtains that adorned the wall.

The velvet material stroked him, gently at first, a caress.

"Get off," he did not like it.

The fabric flapped, tangling around him as he panicked, feeling the resistance of the hard wall behind the curtains.

"But where is the door?"

"Come on," he told himself, knowing that the bald monster could grab him whenever he chose.

"Come on," he tried to make his way around, losing all sense of direction. Breath became faster, a hysterical panting which he was unable to control. Tighter and tighter the curtains wrapped, until in anger he ripped at them, yanking down so they fell away from the rods in tatters.

But he found it. A hole in the wall, the door was open and he deliberately tumbled out, casting from his hand the last fragment of clinging curtain.

He knew the fresh air must greet him with the lights of the fairground. Instead he saw only darkness and with a thump, felt hard boards.

He had fallen through the open door into the shed.

"Oh no." Sprawled out, it was all he could manage.

Twang, twang. Hearing that sound seemed to explain it all. His brain felt twisted. Twig guessed that everything he had endured was a complex hoax arranged by Spike.

"Spike? What's happening? How did you do it? Video? Mirrors?"

Twang, it was all he heard.

"Yeh, okay Spike," Twig was not playing, "I know it's you and this is all a big laugh. And I don't know how you did it but can you light the candle? Please."

A match flared up and then quickly went out.

Twig could hear the scrabbling of another match being found. But in that instant, that burst of light had revealed so many sights. Twig could kneel in the darkness and put together a complete picture of all he had seen.

The old watering can, that was still there, he had seen it. The bench, that was there too. And his seat, the old cardboard box, as crumpled as ever, awaited him.

"But…"

Another match was struck, the candle was alight, showing Twig the remaining piece of the picture. A pair of rainbow shoelaces, a toothless grin, the last piece of the puzzle was falling into place, while Twig was seeing the real thing.

"Crab!"

Twang.

Crab was playing with Spike's elastic band.

No time to move, no time to think. Crab swooped so fast. Twig was caught, held by massive hands.

"Yaheee," Crab was delighted.

"What do you want?" Twig pleaded, recoiling from the stench of Crab's breath.

Crab was ignoring him, intent on his task. Twig felt the air squashed out of his chest as he was pinned to the ground with the grime from the floor grinding into his head.

Coils of rope were produced. Stupefied,

Twig guessed they were the same ropes used by Budge and Spike to tie Crab. Whatever night that was – did it matter?

Twig was tense, the ropes cutting into his flesh, he was being bound hand and foot.

"What are you going to do?" He blubbered, hating himself for being such a coward.

Twig squeezed his eyes shut. Stinging tears were leaking out and dripping to the floor. He wanted his old friends to be there; Spike annoying and Budge protecting.

"Budge!"

"Help!"

No one would answer his plea, ever.

In misery, Twig slumped. Unable to take anymore he lapsed into unconsciousness.

Everything ceased to exist, there was nothing, even the darkness had gone. But something stirred, deep inside. His very soul was saving him, taking him to where he really wanted to be. Walking upward, effortlessly, toward a bright light, Twig felt so much at peace, free from all torment.

He entered the light and walked into his own bedroom. It was dark outside but the yellow curtains were drawn and the center light chased away all shadows.

Delicious sounds and smells wafted up from downstairs.

"I'll bring you up some tea," he heard his mother call. "It must be the flu coming on. Not surprising since you're out gallivanting at all hours."

How nice a mother's nagging voice could be.

"You get into bed," she ordered.

"Perhaps it is just the flu," Twig sighed.

He collapsed on his bed, keeping well in the middle – too scared to probe and investigate underneath, the one place light could not reach. Dark hands of bone could appear anytime.

He just kept well away from the edge.

He began to fall in and out of sleep, in and out of dreams.

Nightmares were not far away.

Being watched. The feeling had been there for some time and slowly rose. He was being watched. Rolling onto his back, Twig raised his neck to see.

Someone was in the room.

A black shape, a blot of ink, the solid outline of Osmomso was at the foot of the bed, rising taller, reaching the white ceiling and spreading out like a great black sheet, slowly descending to smother.

"Mom," he cried the one word that meant so much.

That cry chased the sheet away. It slipped back, twisting down, forming a tall column, funneling forward to the foot of the bed.

There was not a thing Twig could do to prevent what was going to happen.

The last of Osmomso went. Two arms appeared, black shadows, long enough to easily reach the head of the bed. Up and over they snaked, grabbing hold of Twig's ankles.

"Ohhh," Twig sobbed. "Not this again. Please, no. No, no, no."

With no strength to resist, he was dragged down into the darkness.

Pins and needles, sensations came throbbing back into his numbed body…

"How much more must I dream?" He groaned.

A yellow glow gave just enough light for him to figure out where he was.

It was difficult at first. In the gloom, familiar sights seemed odd when seen from the floor. An ant's-eye view of benches and boxes, and the shed's tall roof.

He was covered in grime, from rolling around on the bare boards. He tried to stand and couldn't move. Tied up, he lay awkwardly on his side.

"Aghh," his body was on fire from rope burns. He did not want to remember, he had been tied up by Crab.

Crab, a real threat. His head pounded, Twig jerked in all directions, making sure he was really alone.

He relaxed, having learned to snatch at rest whenever he could.

"Wha…!" So simple. He had been so tense that just by relaxing, his bonds loosened. A snake shedding its skin, he could cast them off.

"So simple." Demented, he began to laugh and had difficulty stopping.

"So stupid."

But he was free, forgetting his pain-racked body, forgetting all nightmares. He was free.

The door opened easily and he fell out. He fell out, not from the shed but out and down the steps of Osmomso's trailer.

"How much more must there be?"

The dizziness of bright lights and loud music greeted him.

With butterflies in his stomach, Twig staggered from the momentum of coming to the reality of the fairground. Almost falling, he was caught and supported at the last minute by strong arms.

"Hey Twig," Budge's happy words met his ears, "let's go."

"Yeh," Spike's greeting came with the slap Twig felt on his back. "Let's go."

"Go?" Twig shouted to the backs of his two friends. Budge had released his supporting hold and was walking away.

"Where are you going? Wha..?" What was he saying? It didn't matter, he was with his two friends. Free.

His face felt tight, he knew it was painted.

"But...?"

He was losing his friends.

Twig had difficulty walking, it was almost a forgotten skill, but elbowing and barging through the crowd, ignoring the startled cries of displaced people, he was catching up.

"Hey, Spike, Budge," Twig shouted over the heads of the people. "What happened...after you had your face painted...I mean, what did...?"

It no longer seemed important. He felt fine now. It made sense. He was where he should be and they were going on a ride.

Budge and Spike were ahead, lining up for the Ferris wheel.

The excitement was beginning to set in. The fair had been there for days and only now was he able to enjoy it.

Forgetting all manners he shoved forward, not going to miss out, not going to let dreams catch up.

"This is great, huh Budge," Twig chattered.

He was there alongside the rails of the ride's framework, paying his money and sliding into the yellow gondola between his two buddies.

"This is gonna be good Spike," Twig nudged him.

He was there, placing his hands and grasping the guardrail that countless hands had gripped before.

"Here we go."

He was there, feeling their bodies side by side, feeling the gentle rocking and upward sweeping surge as they began to move…feeling the tingle of fear returning…

Twig screamed. All three screamed. Only then had he seen the painted faces of his friends, and only then had they seen his.

"This is horrible…" the rushing air filled his open mouth, stopping any more words from coming out.

He knew what they were enduring.

They screamed.

Higher and higher they went, screaming, flying. The ride took them up into the night sky, the fairground, a starburst of orange lights below.

Talons quickly plucked each away into their own separate nightmares.

Blurred recollections tried to keep up with Twig. The flight on the Ferris wheel had ended. He had staggered from the ride and in a quiet corner was violently sick.

His friends were lost.

Only remembering the grass passing beneath his feet, he now found himself inside the fence by the hut. He calmed himself in the night air, letting his senses catch up.

"Can't stay here," he soon knew.

The hut rose to the sky, surrounded by the weeds coiled like barbed wire. What horror was slipping through that undergrowth?

Taking a chance, easily visualizing what could be in there, Twig waded through, making sure he did not lose sight of that shed. He could so easily be lost or the shed could change into something else.

But it became real, the thorns, the nettles, he almost enjoyed the lashing pain.

It was real!

Twig stood at the shed's door beneath a clouded moon. He did not know how many times he had been here before.

His fingertips just touched the shed door.

"What will I find inside?" he calmly asked. "How many times, how long will this nightmare last?"

It began to rain. Water soon dripped from the shed's roof and ran in glossy miniature rivers to form a puddle in the worn concrete slab at his feet.

In the puddle he saw the rippled reflection of a darker world, where tree limbs stretched over the sky to form fingers clutching the moon.

Down and down he saw that reflection, deeper and deeper, world after world, darker and darker.

"How many times," he whispered again, "how long will this nightmare last?"

He tried counting raindrops.

In despair Twig turned his head up to the sky. He saw a few stars between a break in the clouds, and closing his eyes, his mouth silently moving, he privately prayed to be saved.

Rain splashed in his open mouth. It was wonderful, the taste of the water trickling over his tongue and into his raw throat. It was wonderful the rain on his face.

And slowly the rain began to wash away the paint. Slowly at first, streaks of makeup appeared, and the colors ran and dripped into that dark puddle.

And slowly, the rain began to wash away his dreams.

Chapter 13
"Older than yesterday…"

The leaves of the trees around the clearing at grandfather's old-barn house were dying, slowly turning brown with the season's change. The smoke rose weakly from the chimney, having little strength to rise into the rain-washed sky, preferring to curl down to the ground, seeking rest between the clumps of grass.

Inside, in the smoke-stained room, Silk watched her grandfather tend to the fire. He was as wobbly as the bent pipe leading from the stove.

"How old he has become," she whispered. "So much older than yesterday."

"Come, sit down," she called across, patting his threadbare armchair, "rest."

"Ahh," he exhaled painfully. Hobbling through wisps of smoke, he leaned on anything close at hand, chairs and tables. "Ahh. I will soon rest for a long time." His words carried up with the smoke.

"You should not say such things," Silk did not want to hear him talk of dying.

"Wait," she said, "I will help you." Effortlessly wheeling her chair through the carefully arranged furniture, she allowed him to support himself by the handles, and guided him back to his armchair.

"Now, you see," he gently laughed. "Now you are helping me move around."

"It is more than a pleasure," she said simply. And it was more than a pleasure, for her to pay back so much devotion.

He lowered himself, almost falling into his seat and sat there, rubbing his legs with his gnarled hands, closing his eyes, rocking slowly back and forth.

"The dust has been used so many times now," he nodded. "It has weakened me too much."

He was almost singing to himself, "My ghost is calling me to desert mountains, where eagles soar, and where I shall dance my death dance."

Silk openly allowed her tears to flow. "I know," she said, admitting that he would die soon. "You shall rest."

"But without the dust," she heard him say, "my spirit and my ancestors' spirits shall never truly rest."

There was warrior's blood in Silk's veins. It surged through her body, never allowing her to accept defeat. Her eyes snapped open wildly, "You shall have the dust to take with you." Like a wild animal, she growled, "Osmomso shall pay."

Chapter 14
"Grandfather will call for you, tonight…"

"Come on, come on," Spike's voice clanged in Twig's brain. "Get your face painted again."

"No, no, no." Twig clamped his hands over his ears, squeezing out the torment. "Make it all go away."

"Need to get my face painted," Budge swayed in the twilight.

They all cluttered the pavement, outside someone's front yard, by the park gates.

"Need to get my face painted," Budge was becoming agitated.

"What's happening to us?" Twig searched the stretch of park between the fairground and their gathering point. "Can't you see how we've all changed?"

"Need to get my face painted."

"Stop it," Twig suddenly turned on Budge, beating his fists on his idol's chest. "Stop it Budge, stop it." Budge just stood there letting it happen and Twig eventually subsided, with his arms falling meekly by his side.

"Oh Budge," he sobbed, "you were never meant to be like this. It's not how it was supposed to be."

Twig wished in vain that they could sit simply in their shed once again.

"Make it be like before," he begged and raised his head to the sky, praying for last night's rain to return. "It didn't wash enough away."

"What are you carrying on about?" Spike

teased. "Shut up. Don't be stupid and come on," he walked through the gates and expected the others to follow.

Twig searched again the wide strip of park land, it was barren and empty.

"Just like my life."

His shoulders drooped. The temptation of having his face painted began to grow.

"What else is there now?"

"That's right, come on," Spike urged.

"But, those nightmares...and us. And...?"

"Come on."

Spike's hooked finger beckoned, tempting him. The thrill and the excitement was becoming overpowering.

"No," something swooped low between them.

"Oh, not you again," Spike groaned. "Where did you come from?"

"Silk?" Twig gasped.

"Clear off, you cripple," Spike was jeering. "Stop interfering," he waved her away. "Go on, shove her Budge."

"Twig," Silk's words came like machine-gun fire, "Don't listen to him. Be yourself, be strong, it's a drug, fight it, help yourself..."

"Shut her up Budge," Spike urged.

Silk continued, "Help your friends, help..."

She stopped. Budge was grabbing hold of the wheelchair's handles. Silk turned, looking up in alarm.

"He doesn't mean it," Twig apologized. "No," Twig coaxed gently, "Budge, leave her alone."

"Shove her, Budge," Spike commanded.

Budge stood there, confused.

"I'll do it then," Spike ran between them to grab the wheelchair.

"You dare touch me," Silk warned.

Spike backed off.

Twig saw Silk's strength and hated his own weakness. He snapped.

"Leave her alone."

He marched up to Spike, his right arm by his side, his fist clenched. His forearm arched, his wrist curled, and in a blur he punched Spike on the nose. He heard and felt the squelch.

"Ugh," Spike made a strange noise. He backed away holding his coat sleeve over his nose. Blood was dripping.

"You'll pay for this," Spike whined as he ran away, "all of you. You'll pay."

Twig actually enjoyed hitting him, "Never done anything like it," he muttered.

"Twig," Silk was gently saying, "thank you."

"Wha...? Oh – it's okay," nursing his bruised knuckle, he had to let his shattered thoughts piece together. "Is it all over?" He knew it wasn't.

"No," Silk said. "Osmomso's hold is stronger than that."

"But...what's really happening?" Twig searched Silk's face. "My dreams...I wake and I still dream...feel so mixed up. Yet I keep going back...I..."

"Sshh," Silk hushed him by placing her finger over her own lips, "I must go to my grandfather. He shall call for you tonight."

"Need to get my face painted." Budge was moving.

"No, Budge," Twig moved squarely in front. "Come on, I'll take you home. But first, Silk, I…"

She had gone.

"Grandfather will call for you, tonight," her message repeated so clearly in his head.

Chapter 15
"In dreams or reality, he comes and goes…"

The night was dark, but even darker was the dirt road leading through the arched rhododendrons and into the woods.

Twig stood alone, hearing his heart thumping to the faint beat of music from the distant fair.

"Why am I doing this?" he asked himself. "Don't even know where Silk lives. Why don't I turn back?"

Down the lane from where he came, a branch had grown twisted into the white glow from the streetlight. Seeing this, Twig saw, or imagined he saw, a skeletal hand. Spike's hooked finger beckoned him back.

He touched his face and Budge's words echoed.

"Need to get my face painted," Twig whispered. It seemed so much easier, just to go back to Osmomso.

"It wasn't that bad, having my face painted," he tried to convince himself.

The recollection of his dreams slipped to wherever dreams go. The terror had diminished. The creeping threat of walking along the dark road and into the woods was real.

"I will turn back," he had decided.

"Grandfather will call for you tonight."

"Wha…?"

An apparition, a vision of Silk suddenly floated before him, ghostly pale.

"Wha…?" So real, Silk was talking to him but he knew she was not there.

"But how will he call?" Twig spoke as if Silk was really there. "I'm going crazy," he tried to joke. "How will I find you?" The sting of wood smoke filled his nostrils, enticing him away.

"This is crazy." He was led into the woods by a trail of smoke.

Something followed him.

From behind his table of paints, Osmomso fumed at Spike.

"I told you. I told you to make sure you brought the other two with you."

"I tried," Spike whined, wringing his hands. "It was…"

"Be silent!" Red with rage, Osmomso flew out his arms and panted from the exertion.

"One more time," the ogre brooded. "One more painting, and then they will always be trapped by dreams. One more time. And then I can move on to another town, for more paintings."

"Why?" Spike's meek question was just heard.

"You dare ask why," Osmomso controlled his words. "Because I was made to suffer once. Laughed at, by you damned kids."

"When did I laugh at…?" Spike's question faded. Osmomso's eyes were a window to insanity.

"But…but," Spike spluttered, "can I have my face painted though? You said you would, you said you would make my dreams go away, you said, you said…"

"I said, I said," Osmomso ranted. "I'll tell

you what I said. I said to bring the other two with you." He exploded, "That's what I said."

"But it wasn't my fault," Spike ducked away, "that cripple, Silk, she…"

"Silk!" Osmomso stopped him. "That girl." He nodded knowingly, "Ah yes. So, she is interfering. And that old man." He seethed. "Let them try, I am stronger now."

Fumbling with the key around his flabby neck, the drawer slid open and Osmomso greedily clutched the earthenware jar to his chest.

"I have it," he cackled, "I'll see that they suffer."

Osmomso clicked his fingers and a shape slid sideways from the purple shadows.

"Crab," Spike squealed, "what…?" He backed away, seeing a hideous painted face of bubbling spiders.

"So you know Crab," Osmomso leered. "I meet with him from time to time. Yes, I have painted his face often. Yes, Crab haunts everyone's dreams."

"Crab comes just in dreams?" Spike asked.

"Oh," Osmomso gloated, "he is real too. Dream or reality, he comes and goes."

"Crab," Osmomso loomed forward, "get the other two and bring them back."

🦇 🦇

"Stupid, following smoke." Twig tested to confirm that he could hardly see his own hand in front of his face. Still he glanced over his shoulder.

"I've been tricked," his yell trailed behind him.

"It's coming for me again."

He ran up the dark lane. Pursued by something that was so familiar yet so unknown, a returning nightmare, a wild beast of the night.

He stumbled but managed to stay half upright, taking long, faltering steps, prolonging the impact with the ground, only to slam into something hard and ungiving.

Sliding down he reached out to support himself on whatever he had hit. A tree, he guessed, but feeling clothes, he knew immediately that it was a man, tall and thin.

Twig sensed that he was very old. And he reeked of wood smoke.

Chapter 16
"Someone who dreams of soaring eagles…"

It filled the sky. Its smooth, sweeping curve broken up by the desert haze, the last segment of a scarlet sun slipped beyond the distant horizon.

A scorching wind seared over ocher rocks and up the cliff face, bringing sand to Twig's open hands. On a ledge below the mountain's peak, he sat cross-legged on a woven Indian rug. Piled in his hand, the sunset-red sand leaked through his fingers and flowed away, taken back by the wind.

From above came the lonely cry of a soaring eagle.

Twig gazed up from darkness and guessed he had fallen down a well; yet he felt calm and uninjured.

A face entered the circle of daylight above.

"He is waking up." The voice bounced down.

Twig vaguely remembered that face, the wise face of an old man. But that scraggy hair…

"The scarecrow," Twig's words bounced up and out through the opening above.

"He said it again," Twig heard the familiar tune of a girl's voice. "Scarecrow," she said, "I think he means you, Grandfather."

A giggle wound its way down the well.

"But…?" Twig blinked repeatedly and his vision cleared. The circle of daylight opened

79

out. Shifting his position he saw that he was not in a well. He lay on bright colors, a wood-beamed roof high above.

"But…?" He kept blinking, turning his head, left to right. He was on a woven rug on a stone floor and he could see furniture spread through a wide room.

"But…?" Everything was tinged brown.

The stove belched smoke.

"But…who was talking…?"

"Hello, Twig."

Hearing that, Twig flicked himself up on his elbow and looked further to his right.

"Silk…where…?" Dressed in a tie-dyed T-shirt, she was using her fingers to comb her brown hair from her face. She smiled down at him.

"Take your time," a steady voice came from his left and Twig investigated.

In a corduroy suit, an old man sat on a worn armchair.

"The Scarecrow," Twig muttered.

"Scarecrow," Silk giggled. "It suits you, Grandfather."

"Grandfather?" Twig's head switched from left to right, a spectator at a tennis match.

"But," Twig stammered, "Silk…how…?"

"He fidgets and he speaks with just one or two words," the old man said drily.

"It's all right," Silk soothed Twig.

"You ran into Grandfather in the woods. You collapsed…"

"I collapsed," Twig panicked, "I was chased…how did I get here…how…?"

Silk's raised hands calmed him.

"Grandfather carried you here," she told him, "and you slept. So peacefully."

"So peacefully," Twig nodded and admitted, "I did sleep peacefully. But I dreamed…" he stiffened then relaxed.

"I dreamed that I was on a mountain in a desert. Sand was slipping through my fingers. An eagle, it…"

"Ah," the old man interrupted with a raised finger, "he is the one."

"He is the one to help us. He dreams of my death place."

"What?"

"The sand slipping away," the old man's voice was thin, "it is my time running out."

"What?"

"It is all right," Silk reassured Twig. "Here, drink some broth and we will explain."

The delicious smell overflowed from the mug Silk was handing down. He was ravenous.

"You should call your parents," Silk said.

"Mmmm," Twig nodded between sips, burning his lip, "my mom, yes."

"Then we will talk," Silk said.

"There is much to explain," the old man added.

"Yes," Silk said loudly, "and I will explain while you rest, Grandfather."

She turned her chair to face the old man.

"You have done too much tonight," she scolded. "Rest, Grandfather. Or I shall call you Scarecrow."

Silk giggled to Twig. "You kept saying that name in your sleep, and we could not understand. But I see now what you mean.

Scarecrow, it suits my grandfather. But so does Woodsmoke."

"Woodsmoke, yes…I followed it. But…?"

He fought off the panic but he was still puzzled by the night's memory.

"But, I was chased in the dark. I saw you and I…and that smoke, I followed it, I can smell it now. I…"

"Shh," Silk soothed, "nothing can reach you here."

He calmed down, "But why is everything stained brown?"

The old Indian slumbered. His breath was shallow.

Was he really dying? Twig knew, never to ask.

"But..?" Twig whispered to Silk, careful not to wake him. "Was he really a Chief?"

"I can never tell," Silk shrugged, "the way Grandfather answers questions. It is not easy to really understand."

"I know," Twig nodded.

It took many repeated answers for him to understand all he had been told about the dust. There was so much to understand, so much still to know.

Ghosts and dreams swirled in his head.

He shuddered and pulled his thoughts down to earth. He wondered about Silk's parents, but did not ask.

"So are you a squaw?" Wide-eyed, Twig leaned closer to Silk who sat alongside him on the rug.

She just laughed and also leaned closer.

His bare arm just brushed hers. That touch created a strange sensation. Shivering through his body, it was almost painful, but so pleasant.

From the corner of his eye he spied on her to detect any sign, to see if she was feeling the same. He could not help but look over her body, focusing on her legs. In jeans, they were laid out in a curve.

He remembered the difficulty the old Indian had in helping Silk from her chair and onto the rug.

Silk was watching him and followed his gaze and she, too, looked down at her legs.

She sighed.

"Oh." Hearing that sigh, it dawned on Twig what was happening. He was caught. "I'm…I'm sorry, staring at you…I mean…How did it happen…were you born..? I mean..." Twig's words stuttered to a halt.

"I could walk in the air," she was looking straight at him.

"In the air? What?"

"I could walk in the air," Silk swung her gaze upward to the high roof and Twig did the same.

"I could fly," her singing words carried him high into the shadows of the roof and back in time.

"I was going to be a circus queen," she was proud.

"I could walk in the air, across a thin strand of wire. Grandfather taught me. I learned so quickly. It was Osmomso. The dream dust."

"Osmomso?" Twig interrupted, trying to

comprehend too much too quickly.

"He stole the dust one night," Silk continued, "and we did not know. He seemed kind. We did not know what he was really like."

"He tricked me into his trailer. I had my face painted, for fun."

"And that night," she sighed, "I dreamed I was an angel."

"An angel," Twig was entranced.

"I could fly," Silk continued.

"Then I woke. I had sleepwalked. I was alone in the dark circus tent. High, higher than I had ever been before. I was so alarmed, I slipped and fell."

"And now…" She ran her hands over her legs.

"Oh," Twig was in shock. "Oh," he just spoke of his confusion. "So it was Osmomso who did it to you. And yet you help me?"

"We cannot undo this wrong," she waved to her dead legs. "But we must stop Osmomso from doing further harm. It is our duty. Grandfather and I."

"But…but…" Twig blurted. "If he did this to you, what will he do to me! And there could be many others like me and Budge and – why have you never tried before? I mean, to steal the dust back…and…?"

He paused, realizing what he was saying.

"I'm sorry, being selfish. I…"

"You are just confused," Silk reassured him.

"Your story," Twig said quietly, "it upset me. I wasn't blaming you, it…"

"Shh," Silk touched his arm.

"But we have to steal the dust back," Twig was inflamed.

"Steal!" A steady voice intruded. "How can you steal what does not belong to someone?"

"Oh," Silk was upset. "Grandfather, I did not know you were awake. Were you listening to me? I…"

"I only heard what I already know. But the dust," he explained to Twig. "We have not yet tried to retrieve it. Osmomso is cunning and would be expecting us. There is much to lose if we fail only once."

"I see," Twig felt stupid.

"It is not wise," the old man continued, "it is foolish to attempt something that you know will fail. We cannot try until we know the time has come. We need a sign." He stopped speaking.

"A sign," Silk finished it for him. "Like someone who dreams of soaring eagles."

Twig saw. They were staring at him.

85

Chapter 17
"It is easy for one who dreams nothing…"

"Let go of my wrist," Twig yelled at Spike and kicked out, but missed and banged his knee on the bench, almost knocking the candle over.

The only source of light in the gloomy shed, the flickering flame, created a scene from an old silent movie.

Twig felt the upper half of his body forced backward over the bench. Not only was Spike bending his wrist to force him down, but he was also using both hands to turn the skin in opposite directions.

"Wrist burns are my speciality," Spike leered over him.

But Twig had one hand free, and hissing against the pain, made himself fight back. He reached up to Spike's hair.

"Yeeow," Spike screeched, "you're fighting like a girl."

That did it. Letting go of the yellow hair, Twig pulled back his fist and awkwardly hit Spike on the side of his jaw.

It had little effect.

"I'll show you how to hit."

Twig felt the pressure on his wrist released, then the wind was pumped out of him as Spike's fist slammed into his stomach.

"I'll teach you to give me a bloody nose," Spike hit him again in exactly the same place.

"Oomphh," Twig saw the walls of the shed spin up, but really he was slipping down to collapse in a pile on the floor.

"Can't breathe," he begged for pity.

"You're weak," he heard Spike gloating, standing astride him.

Twig lay there, face down, smelling the musty dirt walked in from countless visits to the shed, wishing he had more strength, more courage to fight back. It was so simple in the movies, taking a punch then hitting back even harder.

"Now," Spike brushed his palms together, "when you are ready," he mocked, "we will collect Budge and then get our faces painted."

"Why this?" Twig pleaded to know. "Do you know what's happened to us?"

"What do you mean?" Spike asked.

Something was slipping away from Spike's toughened exterior, just a glimpse. Remaining half sprawled on the floor, Twig could detect a weakness as Spike spoke.

"We're the same," Spike said, "aren't we? There's nothing wrong with having my face painted. No harm, is there?"

"Do you dream?" Twig tested.

"Do I dream? Can't help that…just have to go back…it will all go away soon…"

"How?" Twig pushed his questions harder, "how will it go away if we keep going back?"

"We have to go back."

"Why?" Twig kept up the questioning. "I mean, I feel the same and want to go back. But why? Why do we want to go back?"

"Shut up," Spike snapped.

"Ughh," Twig felt a sharp pain along his shoulder. He turned his head to see what was happening and too late saw the blur of Spike's boot. The second kick was heading for his face.

"Ughh," it scraped over his forehead.

"We have to get our faces painted." Spike nagged. We," Spike began kicking in between words, "have," Twig could only lie there, "to," waves of pain slipped away to numbness, "get," the hard thump of each kick became a splat. He was going to be murdered, "our," Twig felt his broken body resist, he pulled himself up on all fours, "faces," a dog, he looked around the shed for the last time, "painted," as his sight left him, Twig saw darkness spreading from the gloom, "...again."

Twig felt his life slip away, recognizing the advancing shadow.

"Osmomso…" It was Twig's last word.

Twig lay, a boneless shape, his blood a spreading dark pool.

He saw himself. He saw himself from above. So natural. Twig had left his dead body and was looking down, maybe from the shed's ceiling, maybe from outside.

Spike was standing over the dead body, the blood dripping from his boot.

The shadow of Osmomso spread, blood-red turning black, darker than the pool of blood.

Twig felt the pull of that shadow, it was strong, even after death.

"No," Twig flew, curving away through pinpoints of dazzling light and a rushing sea of sound. Wishing to go home, but over the park he flew, toward the rising moon, skipping over treetops and a circular clearing, and the old wooden barn with its chimney smoking.

Following that smoke inside, he saw

himself. He lay on the bright, woven colors of the Indian rug, sleeping, dreaming…

Twig sat on the rug huddling his knees to his chest, watching the old Indian patiently tend to his morning duties with the stove.

"I dreamed…" he was about to call across to the old man, instead he told himself, "I dreamed that I died."

"You dreamed what?" the old man called back.

"Oh, nothing," Twig rubbed his nose and lied.

"How did you sleep?" Silk coasted into the room.

"Oh," Twig turned and smiled. She was radiant in the morning light.

"He dreamed nothing," the old man shuffled closer and Twig had to turn his head from the probing eyes.

"You are ready for the day?" Silk asked.

"It will be easy for one who dreamed nothing."

Twig saw the humor in the old man's face and could only wonder what he knew and what he meant by that.

"You have to confront Spike," Silk was saying, "he seems closer to Osmomso. He may know where the dust is hidden."

"That should be the easy part," Twig gulped.

Chapter 18
"Sweet dreams of dying…"

Hands in his pockets, Twig stood beside the fence in the dusky light.

Like a windup music box, the nearby fairground was starting up for the night. Music was gathering speed, as rides began to turn in time with the chug of generators, and colored lights flickered to life.

Twig focused on the central dome of the circus tent and wondered why it frightened him.

"What goes on in there?"

The wind was right. He smelled the musky taint of the animals in their cages before the show. He loved animals. So wrapped up in his troubles he had never thought to see them, hardly aware that they were there.

"Don't seem to care about things like I used to," he mumbled to himself.

"But why am I scared of it?"

He scratched his bare face and the shadow of Osmomso darkened his thoughts. Being with Silk and the Indian had helped him, he had felt protected in their home. But without them, and being outside, so close to Osmomso's trailer, he felt naked.

The giant toad could draw him in on the slightest whim, Twig knew. He backed away and slipped through the slot in the fence.

The air was as heavy as ever inside the enclosure. All his dreams, all his fears, dwelled there, closing in as he battled through the weeds. And no matter how many times the weeds had been walked through, a path had never been worn. The weeds had too much life in them.

The tall structure of the shed came no nearer as he pushed forward. Tangled stems of weeds spread low to trip him and rose over to swallow him. If he went down, he would die. He had sort of believed it before, but this time he was convinced.

"But, when I'm clear of these terrible weeds," he puffed, "I'm gonna have to try to get in the shed without standing on the concrete slab. Dreams could get me. And what's gonna happen inside!"

"Scared of dreams!" Twig stopped, stock still and mocked himself. A sprung bramble branch slapped him on the back.

It was impossible. Twig became impatient, his temper ignited by the hot frustration of the slow progress, but really because of the knowledge that he may never be as strong as he really wanted to be. He would always be weaker than others around him.

"Urghh," in a blind rage, he rushed headlong, a battering ram through the weeds, stamping defiantly on the concrete slab and beating his hands against the shed.

He stopped. His fingertips just touched the handle.

Somewhere, in the outside world beyond, the sun was setting. The dying rays lit up the sky straight above and reflected down on the moist wood.

Red, blood-red, the door seemed soaked with blood.

"I dreamed that I died in there," he quietly admitted what was scaring him.

The door creaked open and Twig would never be sure if he had pushed it, or if it had opened by itself.

"Anyone inside?" He felt foolish asking.

Gently, he placed one foot on the boards, not daring to hang on to the door in case it really was soaked in blood. He had endured this entrance into the shed so many times, in reality, but worse, in dreams.

"Spike? You there?"

With both feet inside, he stood to allow the dying light from outside to filter gently inside. His eyes were becoming accustomed to the dark, he could see the watering can and enough of the bench and seats to be sure that no one was there.

But someone was behind the door! The alarm rang in his head.

The door slammed shut, he was shoved forward from behind and his neck whiplashed back with a crunch. He did not fall but managed to twist and grab hold of the person who had pushed him.

"Hi Twig," it was Spike's familiar taunt.

"Spike, I..." Twig felt the shock of a fist slamming into his mouth. His teeth cut into his lower lips. He backed away, lashing out blindly in the dark.

"What's wrong, Twig?" came another taunt.

Again, Twig was hit, straight in the stomach. Jackknifed in half, he struggled to find breath, dismayed by the accuracy of Spike, when he could see nothing.

"Ughh," a dull blow to his lowered chest, a knee he guessed, made him finally collapse to the floor. He held his arms out to break his fall and rolled onto his side.

"Just you lie there," Spike was ordering, "and I won't have to hit you again. For the moment."

Twig tried to rise, hoping to crawl his way beneath the shelter of the bench.

"I said don't move."

Twig submitted.

"How can you see me Spike?" He tried conversation. Perhaps there was still some friendship, on which he could build.

"It's easy," Spike was striking a match, "It's easy when you have your face painted. It's all just a dream to me."

The candle was lit and Twig discovered the nature of Spike's painted face.

"Oh my…" Twig felt sick, tasting his own blood from his cut lip.

Red, blood-red, Spike's face and hair was a dripping mess of red paint.

"Gives lovely dreams," Spike was demented.

Twig couldn't imagine what Spike was going through. It was hard enough, when he had had his own face painted, turning his own dreams into sense.

"To business," Spike stepped back, then without a care, kicked at Twig.

"Ahh," Twig felt the sharp pain spread from his hip down his right leg.

"Why?" Twig curled himself up in a ball, to protect himself.

"It's easy," Spike said, "you come with me to

get your face painted. Or..." Spike danced a turn and kicked out again.

"All right, all right," Twig was pleading even before the blow struck his protective upper arm.

He was playing for time, hoping for a trick to gain advantage.

"Oh, spoilsport," Spike backed away. "Just one more good one."

Twig knew, Spike was preparing to run and kick.

"I'm going to die," last night's dream was turning true.

Spike ran and with a laugh, kicked out.

Twig braced himself, but no shock of pain came, only a clatter as Spike slammed his boot into the watering can. It smashed into pieces and fragments fell like shrapnel.

"Next one's yours," the threat had not gone away, Spike was backing up even further.

Twig knew he had failed, letting down Silk and the old man. And he had not really tried.

A shadow spread out from the corner of the shed.

"Osmomso," Twig sobbed. He was going to be painted before he died.

Pale visions of ghosts and dreams haunted Twig.

"I'm going to dream forever," he knew.

The shadow widened, the figure emerged into the light, a heavy shape. Twig could see him clearly.

"Budge," Twig gasped.

Budge stood alongside Spike.

"Budge, your face," Twig forgot everything else. It was gray, painted so heavily that it hid all his features, so that Budge had no face at all, no identity.

"Care for a kick, Budge?" Spike politely stood aside.

"Budge," Twig screamed, desperate to reach him. "Budge, listen to me. It's a dream," Twig tried to picture what Budge was going through. A gray blank mass, living in a fog and ready to do anyone's bidding.

"Give him a kick," Spike was impatient.

"Budge, it's me, Twig. Help me Budge."

Budge staggered.

"That's it, Budge," Twig urged, "fight it, fight your dreams."

"Shut up," Spike was agitated. "Kick him Budge."

"Be yourself Budge."

"Right," Spike hissed, "I'll shut you up." His boot swung back, Twig had no time to roll away.

"Nargghh," Budge roared and shoved Spike sideways.

"That's it," Twig could not hear himself above Spike's yell and Budge's nonstop roaring.

Following up the movement of his sideways shove, Budge leaped on Spike, using his weight to pin him to the ground.

Twig acted fast, instinctively. He jumped to his feet and kneeled on Spike's shoulders.

Budge lay groaning over Spike's thighs.

"Shhh," Twig soothed Budge. Leaning back he tried to wipe some of the paint off.

Spike seized the opportunity and pushed to slide Twig off, but the dead weight of Budge prevented him and warned Twig that he had to act fast.

"Tell me," he threatened with his fist over Spike's head, "tell me where Osmomso keeps the dust."

"The dust," Spike screamed horribly and Twig winced at the torture that Spike must be enduring.

"It's the dreams," Twig shouted to Spike. "Listen to me, it's the paint that is making you like this. I want to help you, and Budge. But you must tell me. Where is the dust?"

"No," Budge moaned. It was he who moved next. Caught up in his own nightmare, he ignored everything and rose to his feet, stumbling blindly out of the door.

"All alone now," Spike eventually broke the silence with a cackle.

Twig balanced himself to keep the knee pressure on Spike.

"I can take you away into my dreams," Spike taunted, "sweet dreams of dying. Did you enjoy dying last night, Twig?"

"How did you…?"

"I dreamed it too, just after I had this done to my face."

"Wha…?" Twig reeled in confusion.

Spike shifted beneath him. Twig toppled but steadied himself, managing to keep his hold, putting all his weight on his knees.

"Tell me," Twig squeezed out his words, "Where is the dust? Tell me."

"Make me," Spike dared.

Chapter 19
"I made him tell me where the dust is…"

Twig sat, half lying, on the rug. He winced as Silk dabbed at his lower lip. It felt as if a golf ball had been rammed in and was stuck in front of his lower teeth.

"It's not too bad," she said and wrung the cloth out into the bowl on her lap.

Twig shunned the color of the water; it was tainted with blood.

"I'll never set foot in that shed again," he vowed.

He flexed his bruised body and nursed his sore hand, gazing blankly at the red dots along each knuckle joint. It was either his own blood, Spike's red paint, or Spike's blood.

"Feel so ashamed," he quietly admitted.

"It is important that you feel such emotions," the old man's tone was weak. "But what you did, it had to be done."

Twig turned and looked up to witness the kindness in the old face. But he was so frail, fading away.

"The more the dust is used," Twig recalled being told by the old one, "the more it weakens me."

Twig could almost see the energy being sapped, leaving the old man transparent, like smoke. He wondered if Grandfather was suffering any of the torment that Spike and Budge and anyone else was going through.

"Twig," Silk was gently shaking his shoulder.

"Huh?" Twig paid attention.

"You must tell us what happened."

"Spike ran off," Twig tried to keep calm, "I let him go."

"We shall try to reach him later," Silk said.

"And Budge," Twig insisted.

"And Budge," Silk assured him.

"I did it though," Twig told them both, "I made Spike tell me where the dust is."

"And now I have to seize it back," the old man simply said.

"We shall do it," Silk intervened. "You are too weak to risk trying."

Twig watched the old man's expression. Nodding, he was painfully accepting defeat.

"But we shall do it," Twig heard Silk saying, "we shall retrieve the dust. Twig and I."

Chapter 20
"So tempting, to be a friend of Osmomso…"

The pungent smell from the mixture of straw and animal scent refused to mix with the cold night air; it just hung around the cages, where deep inside the animals slept.

"Twig, do not look inside," Silk's breath came in puffs of vapor.

"If you do not look at them, they will not awaken."

In stripes, the light from the full moon passed through the bars and shone vividly on the hard-packed ground where they stood.

From behind the wheelchair, with his wool scarf chaffing his neck, Twig stared blankly down at the parting along the top of Silk's hair. His mind buzzed with fear, making it impossible to concentrate. He tried to take in what she had whispered, then pushed the wheelchair forward.

Everyone was asleep behind the drawn curtains along the zigzag line of parked trailers.

Twig tried to creep by.

First a wheel of the chair and then his foot crunched over an empty potato chip bag. He winced at the sharp sound. Nothing stirred, the noise merely entering the sleep of those inside, completing the end of a dream, or starting another.

Pushing Silk, concentrating on steering her, it made him very much aware of the direction they were going, the path they were taking.

White eyes of painted, prancing horses on

the merry-go-round watched Twig pass. He ducked his head, looking away, remembering Silk's words, lest the animals awaken.

They neared a darker area of the fairground.

There was no shading, nothing to stop the moonlight from entering, nothing except the strength of the darkness itself and the unwillingness of the pure moonlight to touch.

Like the moonlight, Twig did not want to enter that area. Nor should Silk.

He ducked his head to be alongside Silk's ear, "You wait here," he breathed, "no point in taking you further."

"I'll go where I choose," she replied loudly, showing no fear, and pushed herself into that dark cloak of the night.

It swallowed her whole.

Her action, at least, made Twig advance. He was concerned for her safety now, instead of his own. He, too, moved forward and was swallowed by the same darkness.

He could still see, in so much darkness. It filtered the brilliant moonlight, as if he were wearing sunglasses.

Silk was ahead, he could detect her and increased his pace to catch up.

She stopped and he stopped, beneath the steps of Osmomso's trailer.

Silk turned and Twig felt her hand take his.

They did not speak but just looked briefly at each other, and then Twig moved ahead, letting their hands slip apart, the last touch of their fingers lingering.

One step at a time, a minefield of creaks, he climbed up the wooden steps in his sneakers.

Alone now, with no one to turn to, he felt unusually brave.

"Got no choice," he shrugged.

The metal handle was cold and hard.

But still he turned it, and Twig was not surprised to find the door was not locked.

Perhaps Osmomso was expecting him, perhaps it was a trap. Twig's imagination was screaming.

With a prod, the door opened a fraction.

Behind that door, Twig was convinced, a circle of demons were chanting for murder, waiting for him to enter and be captured and torn apart.

But still he entered.

Hushed and waiting, the whole room was hushed and waiting. The purple interior generated its own light. A soft glow came from the curtains illuminating the interior. Everything was expecting him.

The bed was at the far end, dominating the room. He walked toward it, but it was the bed that seemed to be moving, advancing smoothly on runners, toward him.

He could see Osmomso, a great bulk beneath the sheets, his bald head on the pillow.

How odd it was, to see him lying horizontal.

Mesmerized, Twig moved to investigate, to inspect Osmomso at that strange angle.

"Huuh," Twig almost screamed aloud. Osmomso's eyes were open.

Twig froze, his limbs petrified in midstride. He held his breath.

Osmomso did not stir, only the sheets above his chest moved, up and down, up and down, in time with the ponderous breathing.

He was asleep.

He sleeps with his eyes open! Twig was shocked at the ghastly concept. But he had to act.

There, the chain, it was there, around his neck. The key had slipped around and was in the fat hollow above Osmomso's collarbone.

Twig fished in his pockets. Fidgeting nervously, his fear turned to impatience. He found the pair of scissors and had to use his free hand to hold the pocket open, to get his hand out.

He advanced slowly, fixing his eyes on Osmomso's.

"If you do not look at them, they will not awaken," Twig heard it, crystal clear.

He turned his head, the rest of his body motionless, fully expecting Silk to be there.

There was no one. Only Osmomso's breathing and the rapid ticking of the bedside clock.

But obeying Silk, concentrating only on the key, it helped him continue.

So close to Osmomso, he could smell the dank sweat. He was revolting.

His hand like jelly, Twig slipped the scissors under the chain.

Osmomso stirred, a snore erupted, he was moving, he was going to roll on his side.

Twig squeezed the scissors, the chain parted, the key...but the key was slipping down beneath the sheets. Twig dare not think, his hand plunged in and was out with the key before he knew it.

Trying to walk on air, not wanting to make a sound, Twig retreated, not turning until he was clear of the bed and a safe distance from Osmomso.

If he woke now, Twig would at least have a head start, a chance.

The curtains forming the cubicle were apart and Twig slipped in.

The jars of paint were laid out over the table, each bold color luminescent. Twig was becoming distracted by those paints. Distraction turned to obsession. He turned the key in his palm, while with his free hand he felt his cheeks.

He felt suddenly tired.

So tempting, to dab his finger in a jar and daub his cheeks. So tempting to be a friend of Osmomso instead of a foe. No fear to overcome, no more fighting to be brave. So much easier.

So tempting just to sleep and dream. A warm blanket, sleep was encroaching even as he stood.

He was doing it, so cold and yet so pleasant, the clammy paint stuck to his little finger. He hooked some out and almost touched his cheekbone.

"No," he violently shook himself awake.

Wanting to wash, wanting to scrub his hands clean, he could only rub the paint on his scarf.

He had to rush, time was wasted. No time to think, no time to be bothered with fighting off temptations.

He found the drawer, the key turned for him.

With a click, the lock opened.

With a click, Osmomso sat up, awake, his eyes bloodshot and bulging.

The drawer slid open.

Osmomso slid from the sheets.

Twig reached inside.

Osmomso walked, gliding in his robe, toward the cubicle.

Twig held the earthenware jar in his hand and raised it.

Osmomso held the curtains of the cubicle and towered above Twig.

Twig felt his flesh crawl.

He turned but did not call out.

The jar slid from his weak hand. He retrieved it in midair and ducked beneath Osmomso's strangling hands.

"Runnnn," Twig finally screamed to himself, but was immediately aware of Silk's danger. She can't run. He flew toward the door, far quicker than Osmomso could move.

He burst outside and did not bother with the steps but launched himself to land in front of Silk. She was already turning her wheelchair. He landed with a jolt. The jar passed from hands to hands and Twig grasped the handles of the chair. Leaning forward, he pushed. The chair sped along, Twig was stumbling to keep up.

A great screech came from the trailer. Twig turned to look behind as he ran. Osmomso stood strangling the air with rage.

Twig still felt chased, Osmomso was being left behind, but his cry, his shadow, stretched out.

"Keep going," Silk must be aware of the pull of Osmomso and was urging Twig on. "Fight him."

"The cages," she cried, "head for them."

"Wha…?" Twig obeyed.

Fleeting glimpses of the sleeping fairground passed by, fading from view. Twig began to stumble, unable to suck in enough breath, he was being strangled, the scarf tightening around his neck.

On the scarf, the streaks of paint he had rubbed from his finger spread, darkening as they dried.

His legs could no longer move, he began to slip down, his hands flopped from the chair.

But the cages were close enough. Silk gave a shrill call. Instantly the animals within burst to life, charging at the bars, growling deep. Flashing teeth and slashing claws, yellow eyes were dancing slits; such power, unleashed by the wild animals, nothing could compete with it.

Whatever was pursuing them retreated, shrinking back to the darkness from where it came.

Twig sucked in the sweet air and could not take off the scarf quickly enough.

"What happened?" It was not until they were well clear of the grounds and leaving the park by the gates that Twig asked.

"Ask my grandfather."

He could be seen, in the glow radiating around the streetlight. Wrapped in his overcoat, leaning on a stick now, he was waiting for the dust of his ancestors to be returned to him.

Chapter 21
"Warriors of the rain and the sun…"

"But I was scared," Twig asked to be understood. "I can't believe it was me who did all that."

"Ah," exclaimed the wise Indian. He sat at the other end of the smoke-stained room, at the table by the stove. Twig was kneeling on the rug and peered across, wondering what the old man was doing. "You were scared but you were triumphant," Twig heard.

"A true warrior."

"But," Twig shifted his position, it was uncomfortable to kneel for too long; "Kneel on the rug," that was what he had been instructed to do. "But I was weak, in the trailer, I almost gave in, I…"

He was getting nowhere.

From across the room, Twig studied the mellow Grandfather. A halo of smoke about him, he still appeared just as frail, but somehow content.

"Glad I helped you," Twig quietly said, but may have been unheard.

"At least I did that much."

"But," he wanted the old man to answer one question properly.

"How did she do it?" Twig raised his voice and stretched his neck. He could still not see what the old man was doing. "Silk," he continued, "how did she do it? With the animals I mean. How did she know?"

"How did she use the animals to help you?"

The old man clarified the question. "Many things are passed down from our fathers," he explained.

"So you taught her…I mean her father is…I mean…" He was reluctant to mention Silk's father, fearing that it would upset her.

"Her father is in another world," Twig was plainly told. "But no, I do not teach Silk all the things she knows."

Grandfather raised his head, like one who is giving thanks.

"Many things are passed down naturally," he said. "The spirits are around us all, to help us, to guide us. Especially the special people."

"Is Silk special?"

"You must ask yourself that," the old man smiled knowingly.

What was he doing? Twig's thoughts swirled. So busy at the table. Why have I been told to kneel here? He was apprehensive, aware of the shadows suspended above the beams in the roof.

"So much darkness," he mumbled.

"Yes," the old man heard and agreed.

"What does it all mean?" Twig felt encouraged to ask. "I see things differently now. So scared. Never used to be so afraid of the dark."

"Your eyes have been opened to other things," came the reply. "But you must confront all your fears. Your worst fears. That is your greatest battle."

"My worst fears," Twig touched his cheeks and spoke softly. "What scares me most?"

Rising in his mind he saw the great dome of

the circus tent.

He had been near the fairground earlier that morning. Not close, not daring to pass through the gates. Just a walk from home, in the fresh air, to meet with Silk.

He remembered. Kneeling on that rug he relived being there, that morning with Silk.

The fairground was being dismantled, ready to move on. Some things had already gone. The place was empty, deserted as if a brutal wind had scattered the workforce, leaving a disarray of ropes and boxes over the route to the center of the site.

The circus tent rose into the sky, a black dome silhouetted against turquoise. Its arched entrance lay open. It was, to Twig, a Cathedral of Darkness.

"What does it hold for you?" From the corner of his mouth, Twig whispered to Silk.

"Almost forgotten dreams, almost-forgotten nightmares," Silk said flatly. "It does not frighten me. But I will be afraid soon."

Twig placed his hand comfortingly on her shoulder and absently fingered her knitted sweater.

"Almost forgotten dreams," Twig repeated. "It is as if I have forgotten what is going to happen. Does it make sense?"

"Yes."

They began to move down the footpath, side by side between the tangled hedge.

"Why me?" Twig asked himself out loud.

"Why us," Silk corrected him. "Grandfather is too weak," she added.

"What will happen to us?" His question floated up to the sky.

He turned to Silk and their eyes locked. A moment lasted forever.

"We shall know in time," Silk replied.

🦇 🦇

"It is time," the old man loudly announced.

Rising stiffly from the table he carried a tray toward Twig.

"What?" Twig was confused.

"It is time." In his threadbare corduroy suit, Grandfather knelt in front of Twig.

🦇 🦇

"It is time," Osmomso seethed and slammed his great fist into the opened palm of his other hand.

He prowled. His gown swishing, he paced his purple trailer and impatiently casting the curtains aside, stood over his table of paints.

"They have stolen the dust," he cursed, "but I still have these paints already mixed."

The trailer shuddered. Osmomso plonked himself down on the stool. With his sleeve, he wiped the grime off a hand mirror and glared at his reflection.

"It is time," he snarled, smile to reflected smile.

He groped, slurping his fingers into the jars of paint.

The rich aroma of matured wood smoke encircled them. Grandfather was kneeling before Twig.

Twig was puzzled by the tray between them. An artist's pallet, it was covered in dollops of individual colors.

"Seven colors," it was all Grandfather would tell him.

Kneeling among so many bright colors of paint and the woven rug, Twig closed his eyes and felt the gentle touch on his face. The paint was being carefully spread with two fingers. It did not feel wrong having his face painted, and he did not want to question why.

"Lah, hey lah," the old man sang quietly to himself, "Lah, hey lah," with his tongue.

And Twig was soothed away, to a great ocher desert, with distant mountain peaks beneath a red sky. And in that place, a soft rain showered down, creating a rainbow that arched magnificently across the landscape.

"It is done."

In his baggy trousers, Osmomso the clown stood.

His face, his whole head, was deathly white. His lips, his blood-red smile, was spread wide.

Such a smile, telling of no happiness, bringing no laughter. Like his sunken black eyes, the smile showed only evil.

"It is done," Grandfather was fatigued and had great difficulty getting to his feet.

Twig opened his eyes, not realizing the old man had stopped and was standing over him.

"What does it look like?" Twig knew better than to touch his face, but could see the pride in Grandfather. He must have done a good job.

"What does it look like?" Twig had to repeat himself.

"The same as Grandfather." Twig was being gestured to look behind.

Twig turned. The air left his body.

"True saviors. True warriors," the old man announced. "Warriors of the rain and of the sun."

He spread his arms wide.

War paint in seven colors: red, orange, yellow, green, blue, indigo, and violet, the rainbows arched magnificently across their faces.

"Warriors of the Rainbow."

Chapter 22
"A Cathedral of Darkness…"

Crushed by the soles of his feet and the wheels of Silk's chair the sharp tang of pine from the sawdust filled Twig's head.

It was not completely dark in the main ring. Lights glowed beneath the circles of stepped seating, spreading an unearthly glimmer, and throwing up weird shadows.

Twig's neck ached. He was staring up into the gloom where the supporting poles lanced through cobwebs of ropes. He was about to lower his head but became aware that Silk was also staring up.

He followed her gaze back up again.

High, the silver strand of wire stretched across the summit of the tent.

He felt compassion, "Is that…"

Twig was going to ask if that was where she fell from, but knew better.

"I don't want pity," she told him.

"I'm sorry," Twig's words stumbled, "I..."

"Shhh," Silk cut in with a whisper. "He is here."

"Where?" Twig's reply was instant.

Being told that was enough. The hairs on his neck rose, he looked nervously around.

"Where?"

"Here!" The boom filled the tent.

"Wha...?" Twig jumped, his head darting this way and that.

"I said he was in here," Silk stated calmly.

A spotlight burst into brightness. A disk of

light centered a few feet in front of them. A flurry, a great whoosh and something somersaulted over their heads.

Osmomso landed so fast, so swiftly, it was as if he had risen from the center of the ring.

Twig stared. A clown had come up from hell.

"Oh my," Osmomso danced in his baggy trousers. "What lovely rainbow faces." He snarled, saliva dribbled, "So is my painting not good enough for you?"

Twig retreated and guided Silk back.

"What are you afraid of?" Osmomso reached out of the circle of light. "Are you afraid of me?" He produced three aluminium clubs. "Or are you afraid of these?" The enormous clown began to juggle, surprisingly agile.

It was hypnotic, watching the polished clubs whirring, faster and faster, spinning in the spotlight.

"That's it," the juggler sang, "watch the shining, spinning sticks and tell me where the dust is."

"Don't look at them," Twig heard Silk's command.

"Ohh, this is boring," Osmomso declared, "Too easy."

One by one he threw the clubs.

Three times, Twig ducked as each spun over his head.

"What do you want?" Twig tried to sound calm.

"You came here," Osmomso said sarcastically. "You tell me why you came."

"No. Why did you come?" Silk responded.

Twig remained silent, now unclear of why he came.

"Not afraid of me?" Osmomso taunted. "Are you afraid of this?"

A conjuring act, he produced three knives from behind his back.

Chrome daggers flew without warning at Twig. No time to duck, no time to flinch, he could hear the air sliced as each just missed.

Three thuds, each knife was embedded in the pole behind him.

He opened his eyes, after he knew he had shut them. Osmomso was gone and darkness took his place.

The spotlight was off. All the lights were off.

"Where…?" Twig yelped, reaching out for Silk and was about to panic. Then his sweeping arms found her shoulder.

Her hand reached for his and he held it.

"Where is he?" Silk did not sound afraid.

"I'm here," the mocking laugh served as an introduction for another spotlight to come on.

With a burst the beam angled through pitch black, following a rope ladder going up to the high wire.

The clown in bouncing baggy trousers was easily climbing up.

"Why not join me?" He taunted.

"I'll show him. I'm not scared," Twig reached behind his back and plucked a knife from the pole.

"I'll show him." Twig was determined.

"Twig, no. It's just what he wants."

He disregarded Silk's plea and ran nimbly across, but soon realized his mistake.

It was difficult to climb a rope ladder.

"Come on then." In brilliance, but surrounded by darkness, so high in the spotlight, on a pedestal on the central pole, the clown frolicked.

"Damn," Twig cursed. He was tangled in the ropes, only a few rungs off the ground.

"Keep the rope taut," Silk shouted instructions and wheeled up to him.

"Push up with a hand," her words were steadying, "and down with a foot to keep the ladder taught. Then climb with the other hand and foot. Then repeat it."

It took a while for Twig to understand, but eventually he smiled, "I'm doing it," he laughed, "I'm climbing."

"Come on up then," Osmomso seemed to be encouraging him. "Don't forget your knife."

Twig concentrated on climbing and clinging to the knife. He did not question why he was doing it.

His fingers began to ache from gripping the rope. It became colder as he went higher. Even so the sweat dribbled down his chest.

"Come on, rainbow man."

Twig had forgotten about his painted face. It seemed to have no effect.

"You've made it." Osmomso actually offered his hand.

Making contact, feeling the clammy touch of Osmomso, a touch that tried to creep all over him, the truth dawned on Twig as he perched on the small platform. He had been lured up to die.

Close up, breath to breath, bloodshot eyes, a face as white as death; and that smile... he knew the real menace that was Osmomso.

"Don't look down," the monster laughed.

"Nooo," Twig did just that. Beyond the dazzling spotlight, he saw only blackness, going giddily down and down forever.

Twig tottered; Osmomso snatched the knife from Twig's hand. It altered Twig's balance; he grabbed, and then, repulsed, let go of Osmomso. Tipping back, falling into nothingness, he managed to curl his fingers around the pole and jerk himself forward to gain a firm grip.

"Bye!" In one slash, Osmomso severed the rope ladder. It wriggled down while the clown untied a spare rope.

He swung away.

Twig saw the white face float off, then come back.

"I'm here again," his breath was foul.

Three times, on a pendulum, Osmomso swung in and out of view, in and out of darkness.

Three times he taunted Twig then came back no more.

Twig froze. The varnished pole was too slippery, it offered no grip to climb down. The silver wire stretched out from the platform at his feet, inviting the only way to go, into the darkness to join Osmomso.

"Silk!" His shout fell away. He heard no reply.

He felt sick.

Then he was caught off guard. A flicker, a humming buzz, the whole tent was lit up and in shock he almost let go. But then he saw where he was, how high, almost able to touch the top of the canvas dome. And he also saw how far down it was, a timeless fall to the bone-cracking ground.

He cried out.

"Silk," he saw her now. A tiny toy, she was wheeling back into the ring, flinging up spurts of sawdust. "Silk! Where were you?"

"I went to turn the lights on," the distant call barely reached up to him.

"Silk, look out!" Twig yelled. Osmomso was advancing, pacing across the ring.

Frustrated, powerless to help, Twig stamped his foot in rage. The shock traveled down the pole and shivered back up. A fool, he could only look down and witness.

Silk spun to face the monster. Her arm snaked out to snatch a club. She timed it perfectly and with a thud cracked Osmomso's white skull.

A rag doll, Osmomso collapsed instantly at Silk's feet.

"Wha...?" Twig could not believe how easily she had acted. So simple, so graceful.

"Hang on," Silk wailed.

He could see where she was going.

"Silk, don't!" he called down in vain.

Silk wheeled her way to the rope, down which Osmomso must have escaped. It snaked up to the pole at the other end of the tightrope.

"Silk," he no longer shouted, but just talked to himself. "You can't."

Holding onto the rope, Silk raised herself from her chair. She was actually standing, her feet on the ground, all of her weight on her hands.

Hand over hand, she climbed without

faltering. A steady rhythm, she came up, her legs trailing limp.

Closer now, Twig could see her rainbow face, her hair flowing down behind her.

So confident, a well-rehearsed act, she reached the summit and slid onto the pedestal on the opposite pole.

"Silk, what…?"

She sat astride the platform and tugged on a slip rope. A trapeze swung down from above.

It did not stop. Twig could hear Silk's hand slap on the bar and she flew.

A butterfly, an angel born, Silk was flying in the air toward him.

She could not reach him in one swing and leaned back to gain momentum. Three times she swung.

"Grab my waist," she yelled as she approached, close enough this time.

Twig could not move, could not step out into nothing.

"Twig," she shouted in mid-flight, "you are a Warrior of the Rainbow. Do not be afraid, grab my waist. Let our spirits guide us." He did it, so perfectly. He stepped out and flung his arms around her.

"Oh," she squealed in alarm, "You're too heavy." She slipped, jolting the smooth swing, "Reach up, grab the bar."

He reached up, lifted by an outside force, grabbing the bar, wrapping his legs around Silk to give her extra support.

Rainbow face to rainbow face they flew, the wind rushing by their ears.

"We're doing it, Silk." He said it to make

himself believe it.

Silk took control, reaching out with one hand, grabbing the dangling rope to stop the swing.

They hung, suspended over the pedestal.

"Twig," Silk was calm but desperate. "I can't hold on for long. "Drop."

"But…?"

"Drop. The pedestal is just below your feet. Drop and grab the pole."

The pedestal was just below his feet, but below that was a deadly fall.

Twig did not drop, he slipped. One foot struck the pedestal, one foot missed, he lurched sideways but grabbed the pole with both hands.

He embraced that pole. It would be a life-long friend.

"But Silk!"

A blur, he saw her hold slip, she fell.

Twig shut his eyes.

It was a long time before he opened them, too scared to look down.

"Silk," she was not on the ground, "where are you?"

The silver wire twanged, Twig spun around and saw Silk's knuckles, white with strain.

Silk was hanging in empty space beneath the tightrope.

"Hang on," there was just room for him to kneel.

She moved closer, hand over hand, and he anchored himself with one hand on the pole and reached out to grab her.

There was no need. She did it herself.

Swinging her body to glide to the pole, Silk pulled herself up and perched, sitting alongside Twig's feet.

"Silk," he shook his head, "I cannot believe what we just did. I mean you…?"

"Our fathers and their fathers," she panted, "they are here, helping us. It is the way of true Warriors."

"We must go down," she nodded to the long rope, suggesting that Twig grab it.

Twig was numb.

She took it and launched out.

"Wait until I am down," she grunted from the exertion, "then follow. Don't slide, go hand over hand, or you will burn yourself."

"Burn…?" He took her word and waited until she touched the ground.

Now it was his turn. He clenched and unclenched his fist, summing up courage, checking below.

The rope had swung away from her chair.

"Silk!" Back on the ground, she had to lie and crawl. How helpless she had become. And how helpless he felt, so far away.

"Wait," it prompted him to act. He leaped, using his legs wrapped around the rope to take some of his weight.

"How did you make it so easy, Silk?" He hissed in pain, with muscles tearing. Aiding Silk, seeing her crawling on the ground, robbed of her dignity, it was the only thing that kept him strong.

The floor was heaven when he touched it.

"Never again," he laughed, nearly hysterical.

"Here," he hooked the wheelchair over with

his foot and gently, tenderly, lifted her in.

Head bowed, she collapsed in her chair.

"Enough," she slumped. "I am too weak to do anymore," she confessed.

"But Silk," he said, "you were amazing, the whole thing. I did… Silk?"

She was gently weeping.

"Silk," he crouched and moved close, putting his arm around her.

"I'm all right." She lifted her head and the tears flowed down her cheeks, streaking her colors.

"What's wrong?" he asked.

"Nothing," she tried to smile.

He tenderly touched a teardrop and it clung to his fingernail. "Why are you crying?"

"For every reason you can think of."

"Sentimental garbage," the snarl made Twig's head snap around.

A streak of blood had dried down Osmomso's bald head, caked over the paint. He stood over them, a knife in his hand.

Twig remained crouched, immobilized beside Silk.

"Twig," Silk whispered in his ear, "It is up to you now. I can do no more."

He controlled his breathing, preparing himself.

"You dare," Twig snapped upright. He walked straight to Osmomso. "I don't care about me. You dare harm her."

"Brave all of a sudden," Osmomso jeered. "You did well on the high wire, I was watching you. We still haven't discovered what you are really scared of though. What shall we…?"

122

"Why?" Twig interrupted.

"Why?" Osmomso leered with contempt.

"Why? Why do I have to show to you what I'm scared of?"

"Why?" Osmomso glared angrily.

"I'm not playing your games anymore."

Not taking his eyes off the monster, Twig pointed up.

"I went up there for nothing, just to play your games. You are nothing now. No more dust. You are a clown who is not funny. Even if you had the dust, I could refuse you."

"You," Osmomso fumed. "I'll make you regret it. I'll show you how scared you are."

"No you won't. I'm not playing anymore."

Osmomso growled.

Twig stood his ground and placed his hands on his hips.

"You see, I know what has always scared me," Twig announced. "It was having to make my own decisions. But no more. I decide what I do from now on. No one else."

"You dare defy me," Osmomso brandished the knife.

"That knife does not scare me. Come on Silk, we're going home." Twig turned away and guided Silk to the exit.

"You dare," Twig heard the warning growl, "you dare turn your back on Osmomso."

Twig wanted to run, wanted to flee. He clenched his jaw and ground his teeth so hard that his mouth ached.

Still he did not alter his pace. He pushed the wheelchair slowly out.

"Be brave, my Twig," he heard Silk's

encouragement.

They reached the entrance.

An insane moan boiled up, filling the tent.

It made Twig turn, not out of fear, out of curiosity.

Osmomso was ranting. He was slashing the air with the knife, crouched low, backing away from invisible demons.

"There is dust in his paint," Twig knew, "Osmomso is living with his nightmares."

The clown turned, dashing toward the canvas sides, slashing at anything he could, chairs and ropes. He concentrated on the ropes, an obsession.

"Ahhaha." A manic laugh screeched from the clown's painted smile and each rope twanged as the knife sliced through it.

"I think," Silk was calmly saying, "that it is time to run. The tent is going to collapse and there is enough weight to crush us all."

"What do you mean?"

"Don't talk," Silk shouted, "Run!"

"Run!" Twig agreed. His feet not gripping on the sawdust, they skated into the night.

A great thump, a great explosion of air, he turned and saw the tent disappearing, revealing the stars it once hid. A deflated lung, it collapsed completely.

And Osmomso's muffled scream was smothered before it could end.

Chapter 23
"Where is Osmomso…"

The crane was late arriving at the litter-strewn remains of the fairground. One or two of the massed crowd had become fed up and left, dragging their whining children with them.

Huddled in his overcoat, the grandfather coughed and leaned on Silk's wheelchair.

"We should go home," Silk suggested. "You are not well."

"I could stay," offered Twig, "I could tell you what happened." He, too, coughed.

Twig felt weak, almost ill. All his trials added together, coupled with last night's late ordeal, had drained him. The autumn air was chilling his own body and he could easily guess how the frail bones of the Indian were being punished.

"No need for anyone to go," the old man nodded toward the gates.

The yellow truck, belched smoke from its upright exhaust pipe. Off the paved road, the driver was having difficulty maneuvering his vehicle. Once through the gates it skidded over the grass. To make progress, the driver had to tack forward, left and right toward the collapsed tent.

The torn canvas lay in a great circle, with the lumps and bumps making a guessing game of what was trapped beneath.

A crane was needed, the fat circus boss in an overcoat had declared earlier. Puffing a cigar, he was now directing the nervous young driver to reverse closer to the tent.

"Left hand down a bit, right hand down a bit, left hand down a bit, right hand down a bit," the boss gruffly shouted.

"What does that mean?" Grandfather solemnly asked.

"I don't know," Twig shrugged and plunged his hands further in his pockets.

"Perhaps, no one knows," the old man gravely continued. "They all just feel they must say it."

Twig frowned and looked sideways at the old man's face. He saw a humorous twinkle.

"Perhaps," Grandfather was adding, "Perhaps such things are just passed down from their fathers and their grandfathers."

Was he serious?

Twig looked at the back of Silk's head for a clue. Wrapped in a blanket, she sat slightly in front of them, aloof. Thinking about her and seeing her so close sent shivers down his spine. An angel, Silk flew last night and saved him. An angel, Twig did not say it aloud, especially in front of her grandfather.

But it was not only his feeling toward Silk that made his nerves twang.

"I'm becoming nervous," Twig tested the reaction of the other two.

"We all are," Grandfather said.

"Yet you still joke?"

"Would you rather I didn't?" Grandfather spoke in earnest.

"Stop teasing," Silk ordered without moving.

"The tent's going to go up," Twig interrupted.

The mechanical arm on the rear of the truck shuddered as the trailing cable tightened and the canvas shrunk together a little.

"I can't believe we did what we did inside there," Twig declared a little more of his thoughts, straining to speak louder above the revving engine.

"I know," Silk agreed. "It does not seem the same place now that it is smashed." She turned briefly to nod and smile. In that painted smile, Twig recognized that she had been through at least as much as he.

He wondered what she really felt about things, and about him. He wanted to know. But he wanted other things answered first.

Is it all over?

Twig had asked that many times before and did not want to go through more disappointments. He felt no thrill with his part in the victory, just flat acceptance. It was his way of preparing for the worst, if the worst was to come.

"Do you think Osmomso is dead?" Twig found himself asking.

Silk turned her head and stared, wide-eyed, up at her grandfather.

Grandfather showed no reaction, except a slight shake of the head, which could have said, "No," or "I do not know."

"I don't think we could have done it without the rainbow paint though." Twig's face felt naked without any covering.

"But Grandfather," he heard Silk asking, "I thought you vowed you would never use the dust in paint."

"I did make that vow," the old man agreed. "And I did not break that vow."

"What?" Twig wondered if he understood.

"I did not use any dust in the rainbow colors," Grandfather elaborated. "What you did, you did yourselves."

"But…?"

"It's lifting," Silk's pointed finger put a halt to further talking.

Twig put everything out of his mind, wanting to see what was beneath the tent.

Like a great fishing net, it was raised and dragged away. Smashed chairs and slashed ropes, heavy poles that had been snapped like matchsticks; the tangled catch spilled out and scattered.

The plundering onlookers rushed in and formed a tight circle, forcing Twig and his companions further back.

"Where is Osmomso?" Twig stood on tiptoe.

Chapter 24
"Autumn will be a lonely time from now on"

The show was over and the park was deserted. Only the discarded ruins of the fairground remained.

With the weak sun in his eyes, Twig stood between Silk and her grandfather, at the top of the footpath, outside the park gates.

The weary old man was shivering and Twig shivered, too.

"Where do you think Osmomso has gone?" He had to ask.

"You have shown that you do not have to be scared of him," the old man coughed. "He has no power over you. So, for you, it should not matter."

"But what about other people, he could still…" Twig faltered; the old man was facing him.

"Where he goes next, I do not know. What he will do next, I do not know."

"But he may pick on someone else, he may…"

"Twig." Silk intervened, cutting off his questions.

"We cannot fight all the battles at once," the old man concluded. "And you are able to decide what must be done next."

"Me? But…"

"That is enough, Twig," Silk placed her hand on his arm. "Grandfather must rest."

"I will leave you." Grandfather turned. "Come soon Silk."

Grandfather turned quickly.

Squinting against the sun, Twig watched him walk painfully to the end of the footpath. Twig did not look away until he was out of sight, soaking up that last vision of his old friend.

"He did not say good-bye," Twig spoke to himself, momentarily forgetting Silk.

"There are many ways of saying good-bye," Silk's voice brought him back to her.

"You sound like him," he smiled sadly.

She still had hold of Twig's arm, and as he looked at her face, she slid her hand gently into his.

"Grandfather must go home soon," she told him.

"But he is going there now," he frowned.

"To his proper home," Silk added. "Where his ancestors are waiting."

Tears painfully burst forth, and Twig blinked them back, grateful that Silk's hand was holding his.

She was smiling happily at him.

"Will you go with your grandfather?" Twig knew what the answer would be.

"I must."

He nodded frantically and words spilled out, "I'll miss you, only just getting to know you. Silk, I…"

"Don't," she stopped him. "We know each other more than you think."

"But I've so much to say, I…"

"Things unsaid, things you always wanted to say, they last longer in our hearts," she told him.

"I think I know what you mean," he tried to

understand. "Will I see you before you go?"

"I don't think we will ever stop seeing each other and knowing each other."

"How?"

"We have our dreams."

"Yes," he gave a little laugh. "I will dream of angels with wings of rainbows." Then he shrugged. "But autumn will always be a lonely time from now on."

"Now you sound like my grandfather. That is good."

"Silk, I…"

Her hand slid from his and she pushed herself away, coasting down the footpath.

"Silk, I…" He wondered what he would have said if she had stayed. Watching her, with long hair flowing, following the same route as Grandfather, the thin autumn air felt lonely.

He did not move for a long time.

"Still something I have to do," he eventually knew. "The old man said I could decide what was to be done." Focusing himself, he forced away solitude by making his task his companion. But he still felt an emptiness inside.

Twig turned and walked back into the park, skirting the ruins of the fair, heading for a solitary trailer where shreds of purple curtains streamed like banners through a smashed window.

And as Twig made his way wearily over the grass, feeling on his back the slight heat from the weak sun, a long shadow stretched out from behind him.

Chapter 25
"A distant laugh creeping
from a dark corner"

Twig crunched over broken glass. The door had been ripped off its hinges by whoever had vandalized Osmomso's trailer.

Its guts ripped out and exposed to bare daylight, the terror and the fearful memories held within the trailer had gone...except for a faint cry that called from a lost soul, and a distant laugh creeping from a dark corner.

It had been easy to walk up the steps and into the trailer. Now doubt was growing.

Perhaps it was because the sun was setting, but the darkness inside was growing, spreading across the floor, reaching up the pleats of the curtains.

"I'm still here," the place seemed to whisper.

"You…" Twig almost swore, "I'm not scared of this place anymore."

He strutted toward the curtained cubicle.

"He can't reach me now."

"I'm still here."

"No you're not!" Twig tore down the curtains. The colors in the remaining jars of paint were weak.

"At least the paint is still here. I'm taking the last of you, Osmomso. The old man said I could decide what has to be done next. I'm taking the paints."

"I'm still here."

Twig denied that he heard anything, but even so he did not waste time, placing all the jars on a tray, rapidly checking that he had missed none.

"Good-bye." Twig shouted, about to leave with his hoard.

He stopped.

An idea occurred to him. At the same time, he saw something out of the corner of his eye.

"Yess," he hissed and snatched up a box of matches, shaking them to be sure the box was not empty.

"Should torch the place," his last words inside the trailer of Osmomso.

Kicking through the garbage, Twig quickly marched in a straight line to the fenced enclosure, to the shed he promised never to visit again.

In his pocket he carried a box of matches. In his arms he carried the last of the paints that contained the dust of Grandfather's death place.

Behind him as the day ended and the night began, someone followed. Someone very large.

Twig had almost tipped the paints, trying to squeeze through the fence.

It had taken many matches to light a fire just inside the enclosure. He had raked dead weeds together with his foot and made a pile.

Now it smoldered.

He held one of the jars of paint, a decayed green, between his hands, pondering.

"What will it do, if I dabbed some on my skin, just a little?"

134

"Go on," an evil whisper urged.

"Nooo!" He lost his temper and hurled it into the flames.

One by one, he picked up the jars, piling each on top of the bonfire. It hissed, and the paint began to bubble over.

He piled more leaves on top and did not want to linger. It was becoming dark.

"Should torch the whole place," he glanced briefly at the shed. But not stopping, not giving himself the chance of thinking too much about anything, he squeezed out through the fence.

With barely enough light to see, he made his way over familiar ground to the park gates, marked by the lights of adjoining houses.

Being followed.

Twig tried to shrug off the sensation, tried not to panic, tried not to run.

He did not want to turn.

Catching up. Whoever was following was catching up. Twig quickened his pace. Someone was following, faster now. Twig could not outwalk it. He started to run and could hear the running footsteps echoing behind.

"Oh no," nightmares were returning. "I'm not scared of you," it meant nothing but still he screamed. The park gates, he rammed into them. They were locked.

"When did they start doing this?" he sobbed.

Turning his back to the metal railings, facing his foe, he sank to the ground, with no energy left to resist.

"All right," he told the approaching figure, "get it over with."

Footsteps crunched to a halt; he saw the person, visible in the glow from the streets opposite. He wore a baseball cap, tipped low over his flat face.

"Budge?" Twig wanted to die.

"Hey," came the calm response. "What you doin' down there?"

"Budge? Is it really you? Where have you been, are you okay?"

"I'm not bad, man."

Budge offered his hand to pull Twig up and Twig became immediately aware of how weak Budge was. He had to do all the work to get off the ground.

"Are you all right, Budge?" Twig was not ashamed to hug him.

"I'll be okay soon," Budge actually hugged him back. "But tell me, do you know? What happened?" Outside the gates, his pants torn after climbing over, Twig still felt the warmth of Budge's handshake.

The footpath beyond was empty, leading down; beyond the summit, the radiant glow from the streetlight rose.

"Silk," he missed her already.

He made his way home, walking lonely streets.

🦇 🦇

Inside the fenced enclosure, the fire smoldered.

Black smoke rose, gathering in one place.

Chapter 26
"Above him an angel soared…"

"Miss you Silk."

Twig sat wearily on his bed and held his head in his hands. His hair protruded in tufts through his fingers.

"Better go to bed early," His mom's nag floated up the stairs, "it's back to school tomorrow."

"School," Twig groaned. It was a lifetime away.

"And the police called."

"What?" Twig raised his head, his mind reeling with a list of possible reasons.

"It's Spike," mom called.

"Spike?" Twig mouthed the word.

"He's run away."

"Run away!" Twig screwed his face up.

"He's probably run away with the circus, the police think."

"Oh…what…?" Twig wrung his hands. "Run away. Never got to say sorry." He checked his knuckles for evidence of the beating he'd given him.

"Poor Spike. What's he playing at? What…?" Twig couldn't understand.

What will Budge say? At least he's all right.

"No more elastic band." He was about to utter good riddance, but felt pity at the loss of a friend. "A pest as well though," he added.

"Put your clothes away," his mom called for no reason. "I cleaned up your room and fixed a pair of pants you'd torn. And I washed your scarf, covered in paint. Couldn't get it all off. It's in the bureau."

"Yeh, yeh, yeh," Twig paid no attention.

He prepared for bed, slinging more clothes around but placing in his mind, the order of things.

Osmomso had disappeared. Twig was still afraid of him, but could be strong if he had to. But Osmomso had no dust and had probably run off to lick his wounds; as Grandfather would have put it. Grandfather and Silk, they would go soon. He may never see them again.

"Never really said good-bye to the old man," he sulked. "He didn't seem too bothered." Twig believed that, and could not understand.

He sadly shook his head and lay down, his head on the pillow. He gazed at the cracks in the ceiling.

"Poor Spike," he thought of him again.

Something else though, something else he had not thought of. It nagged his mind.

What was it? What had he forgotten?

"Hah," he laughed, dismissing the nagging question, focusing his thoughts on all the changes. "Apart from Budge, all the friends I ever had are gone."

"I'll never go in that shed again though. That's definite."

Outside that shed, beside the fence, Twig's bonfire still smoldered. The smoke from the paints gathered, forming a tall column.

Poisonous and black.

Grandfather lay on the rug. Silk had propped his head with a pillow and covered him with her blanket. His breath was as thin as the white smoke that leaked through the stove.

She sat on the rug beside him and stroked his forehead.

He slept.

Beside her on the stone floor, were seven colors of paint. Using two fingers, she began to paint his face, while singing to him softly.

"Lay, hey lah."

Twig stirred in his sleep. The nagging thought penetrated his dreams.

What had he forgotten?

The black smoke crept and drifted away from the fire. A separate being now, not having to rely upon the flames, it slithered over the park.

The darkness of the night grew in Twig's bedroom. It spread from beneath the bed like smoke, forming two arms, twisting and rising. Slowly gathering shape, squat and wide, it slipped sideways across the room to the bureau.

It was complete. Grandfather lay asleep, his face painted with a splendid rainbow that arched across his cheeks and over his closed eyelids.

Silk sat beside him, rocking back and forth into the night.

Twig woke in panic. Either someone had entered his room, or it was a dream. He smelled smoke.

His vision clouded over, smoke formed a fog over his pupils. He could not move, paralyzed by the poisonous fumes.

Dancing before him a face laughed.

"Osmomso," he bubbled.

"You thought I had gone."

"I beat you though," Twig insisted.

"That doesn't stop you from dreaming about me. Doesn't stop the nightmares."

"But how are you doing this to me? It's not a dream, it's real. Isn't it?"

A shadow crept sideways across the room.

"Crab," Twig sucked in his breath.

"You had forgotten about him," Osmomso taunted. "I told your friend, Spike. I send Crab out to enter people's nightmares."

"This isn't a nightmare, it's real."

"Nightmares and reality. There is no difference when I am involved."

"But you have no more dust, how can you be

doing this?"

"The fire, even the old Indian forgot."

"What fire, forgot what?" Twig could not make sense.

"The fire, the paints you burned, the smoke."

"The smoke!" Boggle-eyed, Twig choked.

Crab launched himself, diving for his throat, he had something in his hands.

Twig was given a chance, he could move again.

It was a cruel trick.

His fingers clutched at whatever was around his throat. He felt and knew the scarf. It tightened. His breath came in hoarse rasps.

Fingernails dug in, trying to get behind the scarf. He tore the skin on his neck. Blood dribbled out and mixed with the dried paint.

The pressure tightened and Twig felt his life drain away.

Then the pressure relaxed, just a little, allowing him to breathe, allowing him to live. Just a little, before it tightened again.

Twig was not going to die, he knew.

Outside the sun was rising, red, blood-red.

In and out Twig breathed, knowing he was not going to die, but suffer forever at the hands of Crab.

"It's not fair," Twig wanted to scream. "I beat him."

⋎ ⋏

The old Indian's breath stopped. He lay on the rug at peace. His spirit left his body, rising high into the roof beams, then looking down, smiling farewell to his granddaughter, still sitting patiently by his body.

In rainbow war paint, he flew over boiling oceans, following the rising sun across hot desert plains, guided by a gentle wind to be met by a soaring eagle. On a high mountain ledge of ocher rock, he sat cross-legged on a woven rug and rested. Stirred by the wind, a red dust drifted around him.

Twig tried to cough, the sound strangled by the grip around his neck. Crab was a dark presence looming over, barely seen through the laughing black smoke that clouded his bulging eyes and dulled his brain. Crab kept squeezing, pressing down and letting go, just enough to keep him alive.

Dressed in full tribal clothing, a feathered headdress tapering down his back, the warrior which was the old grandfather's spirit was standing upright on the ledge. His face was alight with the colors of the rainbow.

In his hand he held a bow, strung tight, an arrow fitted. He pulled back the bow in his long arm and let loose the taut twine. The arrow flew through the dawn sky and beyond.

A scream split the dawn and Twig's eardrums rattled with the shriek.

Crab, the dark smoke and the haunting laughter, was torn in two by a streak of light flying like an arrow through the room.

The darkness faded, dispersing into the morning light until, a forgotten dream, it no longer existed.

The pressure around his throat slipped away as the scarf slunk to the floor. Twig breathed in the cool morning air and lapsed into exhausted sleep, at peace.

Silk drew the blanket over her grandfather's head and at his feet placed the earthenware crock containing the remnants of the dream dust. She climbed easily into her chair and closed her eyes.

Eventually she moved across the room to the fireplace. The wobbly old pipe and the gray metal casing of the stove were still warm. She carefully lifted off the clattering lid, and found that the fire her grandfather had started was still alive.

Carrying out her new duties, she picked up the poker, raking at the ashes and stirring up the flames.

The smell of wood smoke filled the room and rose from the chimney into the morning air.

Silk's teardrops fell into the flames.

Morning's tears from heavy clouds, a drizzle soaked the air over the park and dowsed the smoldering bonfire by the shed. With a gentle hiss the fire died and quickly cooled.

The laden clouds did not linger, the fresh morning sun pushed them away. Its golden light passed through the fine rain creating a rainbow that stretched across the park to the neighboring trees, where smoke rose from the old barn in the clearing.

The red desert dust was picked up by the wind and swirled around ocher rocks to mix with the same dust poured from the earthenware crock, now lying empty at the feet of a proud Native American.

He stood on a mountain ledge, his rolled rug underneath his arm, and his face painted with the colors of a rainbow.

A warrior of the rain and the sun.

Twig turned in his sleep at dawn, and in his dreams saw the proud grandfather salute him with a raised spear.

Above him an angel soared.